THE KISSIMMEE PROJECT

MARIGA TEMPLE-WEST

Mariga Temple-West

SEVERED**PRESS**

THE KISSIMMEE PROJECT

Copyright © 2023 by Mariga Temple-West

WWW.SEVEREDPRESS.COM

ISBN: 978-1-922861-48-1

PROLOGUE

Black Forest, Germany, 1935

It was not a beautiful castle. It loomed above the treeline like a humpbacked beast, multiple humps crowned with pointed red roofs like spines down a reptile's back. But the men in the convoy were not interested in architecture.

Nor were they interested in the beauties of nature. The convoy of six open cars bumped over the narrow unpaved track that wound through the green and gold light of the Black Forest, the grumbling engines drowning out birdsong, the buzz of insects and the whisper of trees.

The escort of two motorcycles did their best to lead with dignity as they bounced over ruts and weaved around protruding roots, great, thick, ancient roots, the power of the forest, the still, silent, sedentary power that by its presence alone would hold them back. But the convoy rolled over it all and continued its dogged ascent.

The castle remained half hidden behind its screen of trees, the men could not see the slab of rocky craig upon which it sat. The massive wall and iron gates appeared as a sudden surprise. SS guards were spaced at regular intervals along the ramparts armed with Maschinengewehr 30 machine guns.

The roar of engines quieted to a throbbing purr and for a moment the trees whispered, fluttering their leaves even as the little Nazi flags fluttered with them on the great black fenders of the cars. Two SS guards standing on either side of the gates immediately unlocked them, dragged them open and stood at attention, giving the Nazi salute as the cars and motorcycles drove through.

Passing through a cobbled courtyard, the convoy continued to a second narrow entrance blocked by thick wooden doors and covered with a portcullis gate. The gate was raised by an unseen hand with much grinding and shrieking of metal, the pointed bottom of the gate rising higher and higher as the doors behind opened, giving the impression of a monstrous mouth. The motorcycles had to proceed single file.

Now in a smaller courtyard, the cars came to a stop, pulling up one next to the other in a neat line. The drivers jumped out, each opening the car door for the SS officer who emerged, every one tall, slits of black, a splash of red on every arm.

Generalfeldmarschall von Werther calmly took in his surroundings, the thick walls rising up several stories, more patrolling SS guards on the ramparts above, black silhouettes against the sky.

The five other SS officers gathered together at the center of the courtyard: *Brigadefuhrer* von Weinhoffer, *Generalder* von Schmucki, *Waffengattung* von Bittenbender, *Oberstgruppenfuhrer* von Rottwitt, and *Generaloberst* von Wolfart.

At a nod from von Werther, they crossed the cobbled court, a small army of clicking boots, and up a short flight of steps to one more door. It was a heavy oak door reinforced with iron studs but otherwise unremarkable. Only a fawning doorman guarded it. He pulled open the heavy doors, bowing and bridling at the sight of so much virile power, then stepped aside, remembering to do the Nazi salute. The SS officers brusquely passed through.

They strode through the great hall, thudding over ancient floorboards, the only light from one high window set with stained glass heraldic images. The rearing lions and boars whose tongues glowed red beamed bits of color into the gloom below.

At the far end, another door; another doorman saluted them through.

Then – a vast space. An enormous hall. To the far left on the wall hung a huge red flag with a black swastika. It was the brightest thing in the room. Before this, a long wooden table. The six SS officers clicked their way across to it and sat.

Generalfeldmarschall von Werther ran his cold, blue eyes over the great hall. He estimated the ceiling to be eighty feet high, admired the huge electric lamps that hung down into the room which made the space brightly lit yet golden. Almost cozy, von Werther noted. Directly before him across the hall was a door, a towering archway. Very cinematic, the *generalfeldmarshcall* thought cynically. Appropriate, he thought, to generate a feeling of suspense.

He leaned over to *Brigadefuhrer* von Weinhoffer on his left and spoke in an undertone.

"The woman doesn't intend to keep us waiting, does she?" he said. "Absurd, the whole thing. Coming all this way to see what this female chemist has cooked up in her kitchen."

"She claims to have discovered the spark of life," said von Weinhoffer, "the process of reanimation. She believes that Germany now possesses the greatest weapon the world has ever seen."

"Reanimating animals? Why have animals when you have guns? What are animals to guns? Absurd, all of it. Spark of life. It smacks of the occult."

There was a *crack*, followed by a soft *whoosh* and the towering door opened. Beyond it was blackness. Von Werther squinted, trying to see, feeling suspense despite himself.

Then, from the dark, he saw a figure emerge, someone in white. A young blond woman, Aryan-looking, in a white lab coat stepped into the light. Slung over her back was her own Maschinengewehr machine gun. She advanced a few feet into the room and surveyed her audience with a cold smile. Then she raised her arm in the Nazi salute.

"Heil Hitler!" she declared in a loud voice.

The men stood and saluted as well, crying out, "Heil Hitler!"

"Gentlemen, please be seated. Welcome to Schravenbach Castle. I am Dr. Wild. You do me the highest honor in accepting the invitation I sent to each of you to witness the demonstration I have prepared for today. What you are about to see is the result of top-secret research made possible by the generous support of the Third Reich."

Seriously? von Werther thought to himself. This must be a joke, the woman looked like an actress.

But a second, shadowy, white figure now appeared in the dark hallway and emerged beside Dr. Wild. She was shorter, stouter, a little older, her hair tied back in a severe bun. Even from where he sat, von Werther could see it was bleached an absurd canary yellow.

"This," said Dr. Wild, "is my chief assistant, Dr. Grizelda Rot. The work we have completed here is the result of many scientists working together, paleontologists, archaeologists, chemists, and physicists. And now, gentlemen, behold!"

Von Werther was startled to feel the floor start shaking and he gripped the table before he could stop himself. What was – ? It was the sound of footsteps, he realized as the floor shook at short intervals. Something huge was advancing down the dark hallway. As the other SS officers at the table grew alarmed, Dr. Wild and Dr. Rot stood on either side of the towering door. Dr. Wild was calm and smiling as the thunderous sounds of the footsteps grew louder and nearer.

A small cry escaped von Werther. The five other officers gasped, one of them swore. Just inside the archway, two glowing eyes were visible, twelve feet above the floor.

The *generalfeldmarschall* had to grip his chair to keep from fleeing. This was wrong, some primeval instinct was telling him to *run!* Only his vanity as a man of iron kept him in his seat. His fellow officers experienced the same, abruptly standing up only to sit down again, breaking into a sweat.

The thing approached; von Werther steeled himself to stay seated. Growling and hissing, a fearsome tyrannosaur emerged. It was twenty feet high. The table vibrated under von Werther's hands, the chair vibrated under his backside with each step of the monster. Even the long, electric lamps swayed slightly. It came to a halt.

Brigadefuhrer von Weinhoffer swore, *Generalder* von Schmucki gasped, *Waffengattung* von Bittenbender pressed a handkerchief to his mouth, *Oberstgruppenfuhrer* von Rottwitt drummed his fingers on the table and looked nervously at the exit, and *Generaloberst* von Wolfart went white.

Von Werther stared. He saw Dr. Rot smile tensely and edge away just a little.

Dr. Wild gently rested her hand on the dinosaur's flank.

"Gentlemen," she said, "this is Gretl, a magnificent tyrannosaurus rex, recreated from the Cretaceous period by our laboratories here at the castle. With a herd of such animals and other dinosaur species, world domination is the only conclusion!"

The Nazis sat stunned, bug-eyed.

"Dr. Wild," von Werther finally found his voice, managing to keep it steady. "I congratulate you. Your work is… impressive, a credit to the Aryan genius. But how, exactly, is this… animal… though frightening, supposed to be used on a battlefield?"

Dr. Wild took the machine gun from her back.

"Show them, girl," she said and reached the gun up to the dinosaur.

The tyrannosaur reached down for the Maschinengewehr, took it in its two-fingered talons and pointed it at the table of Nazis.

Noise exploded in the great hall, the hanging lamps swung like pendulums as the tyrannosaur advanced on the table, firing left and right. Bullets streaked across the officers, von Weinhoffer's head exploded, von Schmucki's jaw flew off, von Bittenbender's hat flew in the air with half his scalp, von Rottwitt got it in the chest and vomited blood, and von Wolfart was nearly severed, slumping forward on the table, legs dangling beneath. Great splashes of red decorated the flag behind them.

Dr. Wild, composed and smiling, admired her handiwork through the deafening gunfire. Dr. Rot staggered backward, screaming, shielding her face with her arms. Still the tyrannosaur fired on the bloodied, pulverized SS officers, the barrage of bullets making the bodies bounce.

A volley of bullets riddled across the Nazi flag.

There was a moment of silence. The tyrannosaur glanced over the dead and perceived one still moving.

Generalfeldmarschall von Werther lay half under the table, his spine severed. The floor shook, the monster breathed heavily as it loomed over him. Through his remaining eye, von Werther looked into the blazing yellow eyes of the beast as it pointed the machine gun at him and fired.

CHAPTER I

Kissimmee, Florida, 1941

It was not beautiful countryside. It was flat cattle country. Fences and cows and stretches of grass for miles, hours southwest of Kissimmee. But the man in the Cadillac was not interested in the landscape.

Nor was he interested in becoming such. ...The heat. Such damn heat! The windows were shut against the lowing of cows and dense buzz of insects. Even with the new-fangled air-conditioning the Cadillac still felt close and warm.

The ride was smooth, though, and not entirely uncomfortable. The colonel knew, now, that they were nearing their destination, one he was eager to visit again; purely from a scientific and militaristic standpoint, of course. He tried to repress the boyish excitement that always welled up in him when they approached the gates.

Already it was becoming more wooded. Eventually the road petered out to a dirt track that cut through scrubby pines and live oaks festooned with rags of Spanish moss. Now the trees were thick, a proper forest, the necessary shield. It didn't feel any cooler, though.

The entrance gate appeared as a surprise, its watchtower almost lost in the treetops. When the guards saw the three-star miliary plate on the right front bumper, the car was waved through.

The woods cleared now into a collection of neat buildings and barracks. None of the buildings had names, only numbers, but by now Colonel York knew the purpose of them all. A few people were walking purposefully about. Colonel York couldn't resist and rolled down the car window a crack. And he heard it, his pulse quickening, the weird alien sounds that had not echoed through the air in millions of years, the prehistoric calls and cries held frozen in fossils... until now.

The car pulled up before a low beige-colored building (the archaeology lab, Building #6) where the driver got out, opened the back door and stood at attention, saluting as Colonel York got out. The colonel saluted the driver and headed for the entrance of the lab.

Dr. Wild appeared in the doorway, smiling, dressed in trousers and shirt, coolly elegant. She came forward to greet Colonel York.

"Colonel York," she said in accented English, "welcome back to Camp Mesozoic."

"Dr. Wild," said the colonel, "always a pleasure."

Even now, the colonel didn't know quite what to make of this woman. She was damned attractive, almost like a movie star, and so exotic with that accent. This biologist – chemist? – he'd never been exactly sure of her credentials – looked nothing like the schoolmarms of his youth, not at all the image of a "bluestocking". If the woman was aware of her muted sex appeal, she gave no knowledge of it. She wasn't like other women who might have used it to their advantage. Her attractive femininity was something that just seemed to stick to her without her awareness. Being coolly beautiful without apparent effort. Some women were like that.

Or, the colonel wondered, was that all part of a carefully cultivated persona? He could never fully put aside what she had been in Germany, she that cultivated the Nazis to get the resources she needed. Colonel York wondered yet again, watching her cool, smiling face, was she a mercenary? Was she, in fact, the greatest actress of all, bamboozling a bunch of men to get even more resources here in America?

If that were true, no Oscar in the world could do her justice. Bamboozling or no, she had assembled the greatest team of scientists in the world. She had created her own, thrilling world out of nothing. Like a goddess.

"I am eager to show you the progress we have made," she was saying. "I think you will be greatly pleased."

"I've been looking forward to it," the colonel answered.

"This way."

The two walked toward a waiting army Jeep.

"It's the therizinosaurs I particularly want you to see," Dr. Wild continued. "We've had great success with breeding. I think this family of dinosaur will be the most useful for your needs. The training has come along well, too."

Colonel York opened the driver side door for Dr. Wild.

"What about the tyrannosaur?" he asked.

Dr. Wild climbed into the Jeep.

"Unlike the therizinosaurs," she said, "tyrannosaurs are not herd animals, they won't cooperate as a group." Colonel York climbed in the other side. "They are trainable, yes, but realistically, for large military maneuvers – "

"Just the same," said the colonel, "I'm interested in seeing it again.

"I know they're your favorites." Dr. Wild smiled.

They drove off in the Jeep, away from the buildings and toward open country.

"It's power and strength the army needs," Colonel York said over the roar of the engine. "The Kissimmee Project is a military operation, not just a scientific research lab."

"That reality angers many of the scientists here," Dr. Wild replied.

"Your scientists' personal feelings can't get in the way of progress. The war department is funding you against a possible war."

"I understand, Colonel. We all understand. And you will see today how we have bred and trained the therizinosaurs with just that in mind."

As they weaved their way around stands of trees and over gently rolling low hills, Colonel York struggled to contain that boyish excitement again. The smell alone was all wrong, all wrong because the smell should have been extinct forever, yet it was alive here, smells of living, breathing creatures, musky, unworldly smells, smells no homo sapien had ever known. And there they were! Creatures with enormous necks arching over the tree tops! And there, glinting through the trees, running herds of strange-looking, ostrich-like dinosaurs! The ornithomimus, Colonel York remembered.

The Jeep finally stopped at the foot of a hill. At the summit stood a man in uniform with binoculars. Dr. Wild half-rose and waved her arm.

"He sees us," she said. The man waved in reply and then disappeared down the far side of the hill. "They are ready for us."

"You know, I have to tell you, Dr. Wild," said the colonel, "there's been some doubt in Washington as to the viability or necessity of using these animals in war. You remember you got your funding on your intelligence that the Nazis were developing these creatures for battle. Nevertheless, the military will probably be doing away with horses to become completely motorized. In order for you to keep your funding I have to be able to convince the president that military dinosaurs aren't just enormous, moving targets on the battlefield."

There was a rumbling noise and the ground started shaking.

"See for yourself," Dr. Wild said serenely.

The rumbling and shaking increased, coming from just beyond the ridge of the hill. Colonel York slowly rose from his seat, alarmed. At the crest of the hill, a legion of fifteen-foot high therizinosaurs came pouring over the top, cascading down towards the Jeep. They were bipedal, muscular with long necks and little heads, their long front arms ending in three-fingered hands with sickle-shaped claws thirty inches long. On their backs in special saddles were uniformed riders. As they thundered down the hill, the noise became deafening. They were pouring towards the Jeep as if intent on running right over it. The shaking ground knocked the colonel off his feet and he fell back into his seat as the shrieking therizinosaurs stampeded, the men on their backs urging them on with cries and little kicks until the legion of dinosaurs was abreast of the Jeep, splitting at the last minute and running around it in a great, thundering herd. Gradually, the herd tapered off and the noise stilled.

"They're fast, they're strong and they've proven proficient in one-on-one combat," Dr. Wild said. "A great herd of them is also effective in disorienting the enemy, as you have seen."

"Jesus Christ!" Slowly, Colonel York reached up to adjust his hat.

Dr. Wild turned in her seat and called to one of the riders.

"Captain Atwater!"

A particular therizinosaur bearing the captain of the division trotted up to the Jeep, reining in beside Colonel York.

"Colonel York, sir!" Captain Atwater said, saluting.

Colonel York saluted.

"Captain," he said.

The entire upper half of the dinosaur towered over the Jeep. The therizinosaur bowed its head down curiously.

"They're peaceful creatures, actually," Dr. Wild said, "plant eaters, they have no teeth. They don't bite."

"I can see he wouldn't have to," Colonel York said, eyeing the fearsome claws.

"Those claws are used mostly for shearing off leaves to eat," Dr. Wild explained. "We assume they would have used them to defend themselves as well. I'm going to show you some further exercises."

"Damn! What an animal!" The colonel reached up and patted the therizinosaur on the ribs. "I remember seeing some of these the last time I was here. Where do they come from? One of ours?"

"The fossil was excavated in China."

"Mmm... very impressive, Dr. Wild. Captain."

The two men saluted and Captain Atwater rode off. Dr. Wild started the Jeep.

"There's more I want to show you."

They drove under the hot sun to a stretch of country that was flatter and dotted with shrubs and low trees. Here, a small herd of therizinosaurs were peacefully grazing, munching on the shrubs and shearing leaves off the trees to eat. The Jeep pulled up amongst them.

"We've prepared this next exercise to give you an idea of the therizinosaurs' proficiency in one-on-one combat," Dr. Wild said.

"I imagine those claws would make it impossible for these animals to use a gun," the colonel observed.

"Other dinosaurs have been taught to use them... the tyrannosaur, for example. We have found, however, that the dinosaurs are most effective when using their natural defenses. ...I think they're ready for us."

For a moment the colonel was transported again, so still and quiet was the open land filled with creatures from a vanished epoch. He watched the therinzinosaurs, fascinated, the gentle giants with their monster claws, denude the branches and eat.

Suddenly, life-sized, scarecrow-like effigies fashioned from hemp in Nazi uniform dropped from the trees, suspended above the ground by ropes. The therizinosaurs snapped to, rigid, their heads jerking like alarmed birds. Then, shrieking and hissing, they fell upon the effigies with ferocity, tearing them with their claws, hemp arms and legs sheared clean off, uniforms shredded. Nazi armbands became confetti fluttering away on the wind. When the effigies were reduced to unrecognizable piles of tangled hemp, only then did the therizinosaurs desist, and turned away panting, regrouping, and resumed grazing.

Dr. Wild smiled proudly.

"They've been conditioned to attack anything in a Nazi uniform," she said.

"Charming," Colonel York said. "But one bullet to the head would put a stop to them."

"As it would a man. These animals were never intended to be army tanks. If used in war, many will die like any soldier. It is your decision, of course, as to their practicality. I can only show you what they can do."

"Let's look at the T. rex."

Dr. Wild started the Jeep and turned from the field. Traveling some distance across the landscape, Colonel York caught glimpses of ornithomimus twinkling through the tall grass and darting around trees. It was, he thought, like being on a prehistoric safari. His imagination barreled ahead; perhaps when he was retired, he could run such a place, take families on tours in old army Jeeps like this one, pointing out with authority the different species of dinosaurs, explaining their behaviors with the same calm confidence as Dr. Wild. ...Perhaps he would hire Dr. Wild for his project; he would need someone like this....

The smell... every primeval cell in his body said, Stop! Go back! But the Jeep went doggedly forward and the smell increased... that peculiar musk... the overpowering scent of dung. The very air seemed to change. They were entering a territory not their own, intruders, foolish intruders. But deeper they went into the miasma of musk and dung and some unseen presence. This, the colonel thought, was how the knights of ancient myth felt, approaching the dragon's lair.

He was a soldier, a military man, yet no amount of training could ever inure him to the thrill of terror he always felt when coming here. And it was a thrill. He gave a sidelong squint at the woman next to him, so feminine and fragile in her linen blouse and neat blond bun. She was not afraid. He knew, of course, the stories about her. She could control a tyrannosaurus rex... could face down a passel of SS commanders. But she was a scientist. That was the key, Colonel York supposed. No military prowess was a match for scientific knowledge. There, he realized, lay the power.

But Colonel York gazed straight ahead, gripping the door of the Jeep, stoic.

They drove following a stream, the land was wetter here, and the colonel recognized a particular stand of cypress trees. They drove as close as they dared and stopped.

It was very quiet. There were birds in the distance but otherwise this was a place where the creature ruled alone. In the foreground, protruding through the grass, bones were visible, entire exposed ribcages of cattle carcasses.

"We don't want to get too close," Dr. Wild said.

"I thought you could control these animals," said the colonel.

"In a more controlled environment, yes, but this one we have wanted to observe in as natural a setting as possible."

"How many do you have?"

"Just one."

"Still only one?"

"We had only one fossil to work with. We have not yet started a breeding program, we don't have a female. I assure you, Colonel, it is my professional opinion that this is not the dinosaur for the military. It would take a number of years to reach its full size and the tyrannosaur cannot work as a group. If you want to prevent them from eating your own men you would have to keep them constantly fed with huge amounts of meat which is expensive and impractical." The ground started trembling slightly. "There it is."

About a hundred yards away, the tip of the snout slid out from behind the cypress trees followed by the enormous head. Even from a distance Colonel York and Dr. Wild could see the cruel fangs hanging from the creature's jaws. The beast kept coming, the neck, the muscled torso with its weird little grappling-hook arms. Each step made the earth shudder; the helpless little army Jeep shuddered with it. And still the vision of the tyrannosaur continued like a slow-moving train, the hind quarters, thick as ancient tree trunks, the tail as thick as a man is tall.

Colonel York could hear its slow, heavy breathing. The tyrannosaur turned its huge head and spied them, its tiny eyes two dots of intelligence and brilliantly yellow.

As before, Colonel York experienced the thrill of standing on the edge of death, staring into the living eyes of a monster that could be upon them in three strides, could crunch the Jeep in two like a twig. No ancient cellular memory in a homo sapien could respond to a moment such as this, it wasn't meant to be, time had crashed into time, logic and science upended and yet they were looking into the eyes of a creature that had walked a birthing earth that was volcanic, hot, as the continents ripped apart.

Still, the tiny, hairless, homo sapien's prehistoric instincts don't fail it entirely and every cell was screaming, *RUN!*

"Impressive creature," Colonel York said, sweating the wrong kind of sweat, not the wet sweat of the Florida sun but the sticky sweat of fear.

"Yes," Dr. Wild replied.

"And you say they're untamable?"

"They are unpredictable."

"But you had one; in Germany."

"Yes."

"You trained that one. We've all heard the famous story of what your tyrannosaur did to those SS commanders."

"Gretl and I had a special bond. But even with her, I had to keep her fed. And I could never be sure how she would behave around others besides me."

"Mmm…"

The tyrannosaur stood very still, staring at the Jeep. The reeking carcasses reminded the colonel not just what the dinosaur could do but what it would take to keep it appeased. The creature began slowly advancing, nosing about a little among the cattle bones.

"It would be difficult to transport an animal like that," he said.

"Yes," Dr. Wild agreed.

"I take it he's been fed. No chance he'll be charging us?"

"I hope not."

"I'd still like to see a breeding program with these animals. Any possibility of getting a female?"

"Our archaeologists are out in the field every day. We can never predict exactly what they'll find."

"Is your team reanimating anything now?"

"Nothing at the moment. We haven't really needed to. The dinosaurs are breeding well on their own."

The ground was increasingly shuddering as the tyrannosaur, curious, came nearer.

"Shall we return?" Dr. Wild suggested.

"Good idea."

The Jeep pulled away. Colonel York steeled himself not to look over his shoulder even as the ground continued to tremble and nightmarish visions of monster teeth descending upon them clouded his mind.

As they drew further away from tyrannosaur territory and the air palpably calmed again, Colonel York experienced the delicious sense of relaxation which comes after prolonged tension and he basked in the pleasure of having seen that miracle of a lost age. Now that he was away from it, ideas danced through his mind again of a dinosaur zoo, how one might contain a tyrannosaur, the feasibility of it; but oh! The wonder of it!

The Jeep pulled to a stop among the buildings of Camp Mesozoic. Behind them loomed a huge, hangar-like building. The Lab. Not the archaeology lab, not the chemistry lab, The Lab, where It happened. (Known colloquially among the camp residents as the Resurrection Lab. Building #12).

"What really goes on in there, Doc?" He indicated the building with his head.

"Like I said, nothing at the moment," Dr. Wild replied.

"All top secret. A war would change that. Washington would demand to know your secret formula."

"Washington understood my conditions. If the formula for *Dinolebhaftigkeit* were to fall into enemy hands, the results would be incomprehensible. My team does their work and only I can... reanimate life. Anyway, there isn't any formula."

"So, what is it?"

Dr. Wild climbed out of the Jeep.

"The fossils hold memory," she said. Colonel York also exited the Jeep. "Come to the canteen and have something to drink before you go back. Now there is a formula, my own, for coffee."

"Delighted!"

CHAPTER II

Dr. Robert Gorman and Dr. Alfred Dickhart were finishing up lunch. Sometimes, Gorman thought, Dr. Dickhart was a bit much. He babbled in that rather excessively jolly tone, with lots of British "Rightos!" and "Jolly goods!" and "chaps".

"I'm not your "chap"," Gorman inwardly muttered, glowering down into his coffee. "What was Dickhart babbling on about now? …Cricket? Seriously? Was there any English guy who wasn't fixated on cricket? What the hell was cricket anyway? Some kind of bastardized baseball…."

Dickhart rattled his newspaper (or cricket report, whatever the hell it was), bleating out scores like Gorman cared. Gorman sometimes had to wonder how Dickhart got the job of head archaeologist at Camp Mesozoic. In all fairness, though, Gorman had to admit that the Brit knew his stuff, he came highly recommended from a dig in Iraq.

Glancing across the large room full of long tables, Gorman saw *Frau Dino* and her military lapdog enter the canteen. The world went a little darker and quieter and even Dickhart was momentarily drowned out. There she went, all smug smiles, pouring the colonel coffee like a good *hausfrau*. Boy, did she have him wrapped around her little finger.

Gorman stayed out of it. He refused to have anything to do with the military, would not speak to any of them when they visited the camp. Gorman even kept silent on his suspicions that *Frau Dino* was passing secrets to the Nazis, that she used her cool sex appeal to bewitch men into giving her what she wanted, whether they were Nazis or Americans.

But… she was damn smart. Gorman had to give her that. You had to hand it to a woman who could reanimate dinosaurs. *Dinoleb… Dinolieben…* Gorman still hadn't learned how to say it. Maybe it wasn't even a real word. Wouldn't that be just typical of Elsa, always tricky, always elusive, never revealing her secrets. Not like a scientist at all, never published any scholarly papers. Who would trust a woman like this? She was more like a witch.

Glowering, Gorman sipped his coffee.

It was delicious. It was Elsa's own special brew. Good, strong, black, German coffee. It woke him up in the morning, it perked him up in the afternoon. A few sips of it, and an academic problem that had been confounding him suddenly came untangled. A gloomy day would get brighter. This coffee, it was nothing like the brown swill Americans drank. You could win the war on this stuff alone.

Maybe she spiked it with something. Gorman eyed his cup dubiously. Maybe they were all drugged.

Don't come over here, Gorman prayed. Don't come over here, don't sit with us.

Elsa approached the table.

"Colonel, you remember our chief archaeologist," she said brightly. "Dr. Dickhart."

"Good to see you again, Colonel!" Dr. Dickhart, very jolly. Blond and boyish, he reached over to shake hands.

"And our head of paleontology," Dr. Wild indicated Gorman, "Dr. Robert Gorman."

Dr. Robert Gorman, a man in his late thirties with dark hair and eyes, tanned from the sun was not jolly. He shook hands grudgingly.

"I commend you on your wonderful set-up here, Dr. Wild," Colonel York said, sitting at the table. "You've done great things."

"I work with a brilliant team of people. I have been extremely lucky. The opportunities I've been given here are what most scientists can only dream of."

"That's the irony of war."

"When the war in Europe is over, I hope the United States will continue to see the importance of continuing our work here."

"That's not for me to say."

Gorman abruptly got up and left the table. Dr. Wild looked after him, bewildered.

"Excuse me, Colonel," she said.

She too left the table and went after Dr. Gorman, following him outside where he was rapidly walking away from the canteen. She caught up to him and grabbed his arm.

"What do you think you're doing?" she said. "That was Colonel York!"

"I know who he is."

"Your pointed rudeness to him is not in our best interests."

"I'm a scientist, not a mercenary."

"I don't know what you mean."

"You don't need an explanation, *Doctor*. We all know what you are."

"I beg your pardon!"

Gorman pulled away from her and walked in the opposite direction.

"I find your kissing-up nauseating," he said as Dr. Wild still followed him. "Why don't you just do your job and stop pretending? You're not fooling anybody."

"Ever since you've come to work here you've been nothing but a black cloud!"

Gorman stopped.

"Are you dissatisfied with my work?" he said.

"That's not what I meant."

"Then we have nothing more to say." Dr. Gorman resumed walking.

"I think we do. If your disagreeableness is going to jeopardize the future of Camp Meso –"

Gorman stopped again.

"Disagreeableness?" he said. *"Disagreeableness?* You really don't get it, do you?"

"Tell me! Let's have it out!"

Gorman didn't answer and continued walking as Dr. Wild charged after him.

"Under normal circumstances I'd tell you to leave," she said, "leave if you want to. But we need you."

"I'm here for the research, for scientific advance. Nothing more. I don't have any agenda."

"None of us has an agenda. I had to get the war department behind us, where else was I supposed to get the money? I had to convince Washington it was in its best interests to fund us, even if it meant scaring them with the threat of war. How else could I have done it? Who else could have given us all this? You should be thanking me, times are difficult. We all remember how it was just a few years ago."

"Yes." Dr. Gorman looked down at her. "I know how it was just a few years ago, when you worked for the Nazis!"

Again, Gorman turned from her. Dr. Wild was speechless for a moment and then once more came after him.

"That's it then," she said. "You think I'm one of them."

"I know the facts."

"You know nothing! They forced me! You've never even been to Germany, you have no idea how things really are! Will you stop walking!" She grabbed his arm again and forced him to stop. "Shall I tell you then?"

"I'm really not interested in your version of –"

"No, I'm going to tell you, since you insult me so!"

"An insult? I'm sorry if you don't like hearing the truth."

"Everything I did after 1933, *everything,* was a plot to get out of there. I had a reputation, even as a woman, my name was respected and when the Nazis came to power, they were looking for scientists, they wanted new weapons. I had discovered the process of *Dinolebhaftigkeit*, I was valuable to them. Do you have any idea what happens to people who say no to Hitler? You're lucky if you're imprisoned!"

"Spare me your histrionics," Dr. Gorman said calmly. "Your plan went wrong, your own creation ran amok on you. That's the only reason you left Germany, the only reason you're feigning loyalty to us now."

"Left Germany! I barely escaped with my life! I made a statement, a statement for the whole world to see, especially all of Germany. Everything that happened I planned."

"You say that now."

"I somehow think, Dr. Gorman, that you wouldn't be speaking this way to me if I were a man."

Gorman turned away and this time Dr. Wild did not follow him.

She was standing approximately in front of the canteen when Colonel York and Dr. Dickhart emerged and joined her.

"A little temperamental?" Colonel York said, looking after Dr. Gorman.

"Something like that," Dr. Wild murmured.

"Do you want me to speak to him?" Dr. Dickhart asked.

"No, let him go." She turned to Colonel York. "I apologize for Dr. Gorman. He cares deeply about the work we do here, he hates that our dinosaurs will be used by the military."

They walked towards the colonel's waiting car.

"I don't think your paleontologist fella really understands the gravity of the situation," Colonel York said. His driver opened the car door. "If Germany is also developing this science...."

"They are," said Dr. Wild, "but they will never succeed."

"Our intelligence hasn't found any evidence of German dinosaurs...."

"And you never will," said Dr. Dickhart. He placed a hand on Dr. Wild's shoulder. "Only Dr. Wild knows the means of *Dinolebhaftigkeit*. Germany will never have a dinosaur."

CHAPTER III

Berlin, Prinz Albrechtstrasse, 1941

The woman made muted sounds of protest as she was half-carried, half dragged down the cellar stairs. The two SS guards pulled her across the floor towards a wall that bore the ominous inscription, *Breathe deeply and quietly.* Before the wall, she beheld her interrogators.

It brought back unpleasant memories... a line of SS officers sitting behind a table. The last time... images crowded her fuddled brain. Blood... spattering blood. Noise--

The officers gazed upon the woman with sneering disgust. She was bedraggled, thin, clad in the rumpled gray of the women's prison uniform, her matted black hair hanging over her face in strings. The guards pushed her forward and she stepped uncertainly into the light.

"Fraulein Rot," said Heinrich Himmler with jovial irony, "welcome to Gestapo headquarters. I am Commandant Heinrich Himmler, *Reichsfuhrer*, head of the SS. This," he indicated the man on his left, "is Herr Albert Speer, *reichsminister* for armaments and munitions. And," he nodded towards the man on his right, "Colonel Schumann, our head of weapons research. *Generalfeldmarschall* von Werther I believe you already know."

Generalfeldmarschall von Werther, seated on one end, sat lop-sidedly in a wheelchair, immobile, his uniform bunched untidily around a depleted body, the dark sunglasses like black eye sockets. He might have been dead but for the little puffs of breath that stirred the black silk handkerchief tied around his face.

"Gentlemen..." Dr. Rot said hesitantly, "it is an honor."

"I will come straight to the point, fraulein," Himmler resumed. "The British are bombing our cities and Germany needs to win the war quickly. For this we need a weapon which will give the Third Reich an unsurpassed advantage. Colonel Schumann has recommended you."

"Colonel Schumann...?"

"Meanwhile, Herr Speer and I have been corresponding as to whether or not to release you from prison."

"I see...."

"Naturally, since the debacle at Schravenbach Castle six years ago your loyalty to the Third Reich has been called into question."

"No, no! I have always had nothing but unswerving devotion to the Fuhrer!"

"Silence, woman!"

"Have you never wondered, fraulein," Speer interjected, "why you were not immediately shot for your collaboration with the traitor Elsa Wild?"

"I was no collaborator," Dr. Rot said emphatically.

"Colonel Schumann is aware of your value," Speer continued. "You have him to thank for preserving your hide all these years. There was some question that your knowledge of *Dinolebhaftigkeit* might be useful to the Third Reich, especially if other efforts in weapon building failed."

The black handkerchief over von Werther's face began puffing more animatedly.

"The bomb!" von Werther's voice was weak but emphatic.

"*Generalfeldmarschall* von Werther is, not surprisingly, opposed to the *Dinolebhaftigkeit* of any more dinosaurs," Speer said. "We have included him here today to hear his side of the debate."

Dr. Rot looked at von Werther in horror.

"As the sole survivor and witness to the rampage of the tyrannosaur," Speer went on, "anything he has to say on the matter is important to us."

"The bomb!" von Werther gasped. "Build the bomb!"

"*Generalfeldmarschall* von Werther is in favor of continuing research into nuclear fission," Himmler said. "There is a belief in some circles that a bomb of such power could be produced that would ensure Germany's world domination."

"The bomb! The bomb!" von Werther pleaded.

"The fact is," said Colonel Schumann, "even if this were possible, the completion of such a weapon is at least two years away. Germany must have a weapon now."

"Build the bomb!" von Werther's handkerchief puffed emphatically. "One good bomb... take out a whole city... drop *one bomb*, the war is over."

"What *Generalfeldmarschall* von Werther says is true," said Himmler, "a bomb would be most efficient but it does *us* no good if we have to wait years."

"Yes... yes, I understand," said Dr. Rot. "You want me to build that weapon for you. The dinosaurs!"

"The bomb!" von Werther cried weakly.

"Can you do it, Fraulein Rot?" Himmler demanded.

"Oh yes! Yes! Let me reassemble my team, we'll reopen Schravenbach Castle –"

"Do you possess the formula for *Dinolebhaftigkeit*?" said Speer.

"There – there isn't a formula as such, but I was Dr. Wild's right arm, I know everything, more than she realized. I – I can create anything you wish!"

"Why not men?" said Colonel Schumann. "Why not reanimate men? We could have a perpetually recycled army."

"That – that would be... rather complicated...." Dr. Rot said.

"You can't do it?" said Schumann.

"Yes, of course, it could be done. But... men have free will. The human psyche is too complex."

"Could you create an army of tyrannosaurs?"

"Yes, Herr Speer. With a breeding program you can have as many tyrannosaurs as you like. ...What happened to Gretl?"

"Dead," said Himmler. "Shot."

"Oh. The body is somewhere?"

"In a ravine near Schravenbach Castle," Himmler told her.

"I will need it," she said. "It must be found at once. There are other fossils at the castle, our paleontologists were assembling a second tyrannosaurus at the time of – I mean – at the time Dr. Wild was there. It was believed to be a male. Give me my team and we will reassemble the equipment at once. We will reanimate Gretl and the second tyrannosaur and then start a breeding program."

At the table, the men turned to one another in excitement. Von Werther moaned.

"...no..." he said weakly, "no rampaging dinosaurs...."

"Can these creatures be controlled, fraulein?" Himmler asked.

"Yes. Absolutely," Dr. Rot said. "They are supremely trainable. What Dr. Wild's tyrannosaur did to the Nazi commanders was a perfect example. ...I mean, Dr. Wild planned that, she trained Gretl to do that. You can train a tyrannosaur to do anything you want. Naturally, our dinosaurs, *my* dinosaurs, will be trained to kill the enemy."

"You sound as though you had for-knowledge of Fraulein Wild's plan," Himmler said.

"No! No! Dr. Wild wanted to destroy the program, don't you see? Only she was secretive, no one knew, not even myself until the moment – no doubt she wanted Gretl to kill me too, it was a miracle I escaped!" The men at the table were silent, dubious. "She – she never even wore an armband! Give me one! Give me one and I will wear it proudly!"

"Prove your loyalty to the Third Reich by having a breeding pair of tyrannosaurs ready for exhibition within the year," Speer told her.

"Consider it done, Herr Speer."

"Then you are a free woman," Himmler said. "Everything you need will be provided for you."

Dr. Rot's posture straightened and her eyes grew brighter.

"Avail yourself, Fraulein Rot," said Speer.

"My name," Dr. Rot said, eyes eerily aglow, "... is *Doktor* Rot!"

CHAPTER IV

Kissimmee, Florida. December, 1941

It was twilight at Camp Mesozoic. Dr. Wild stood among the herd of therizinosaurs and let herself be lost in the peace. The air was thick with the sound of crickets, the sky was turning orange and the therizinosaurs grazed on the trees. Elsa's heart was full to bursting. She looked at the orange sky and wondered if that had been the color over Pearl Harbor as the flaming ships had keeled and sunk. It was the clarion call. It was time. And now Elsa was responsible, she was sending her beautiful animals into battle, they had been bred for it, trained for it. She had brought them alive for science. And, she admitted, for a long held desire held by many others as well, simply to see these beasts walk the earth again. And she had done it. Not just her, no, there were many others who had contributed to the knowledge, so many trapped in the imploding cauldron of Germany. She had made it to America, the resources she had been given here were what most scientists could only imagine. But at what price? She knew the price, had secretly hoped it would never come to this. Now her scientific masterpiece, grazing in oblivious innocence all around her, would be machine-gunned, bombed, burned.

"I'm sorry," she whispered to her animals. "Forgive me."

Even now President Roosevelt's words echoed in her mind. "December 7, 1941 a date which will live in infamy..."

The Camp Mesozoic community had gathered in the lounge, sitting in silence around the radio.

"...I regret to tell you that very many American lives have been lost..."

The litany that then followed:

"...Last night Japanese forces attacked Guam. Last night Japanese forces attacked the Philippine Islands. Last night the Japanese attacked Wake Island. And this morning the Japanese attacked Midway Island."

Her therizinosaurs would go to all these places, loaded onto ships, fed and cared for, until the hour they were saddled up and taken to the slaughter. The beasts were untested, their valor – the success of this whole scientific undertaking – was still not assured. If it was a disaster... Dr. Wild broke into a cold sweat at the thought. She would be imprisoned as a saboteur, a spy, a tool of the *Fuhrer*.

It must succeed. The irony was not lost on her. War money had funded her research but the thing she dreaded most was using her greatest scientific achievement successfully in war, thus destroying the very fruits of her labor. For a moment Elsa wished she had never come to America, had gone underground instead, joined the resistance in Germany.

But it was too late. She had fled war; and the war had found her.

Elsa stripped some leaves off a live oak tree and hand-fed the dinosaur closest to her. She stroked its neck as it munched out of her hand.

I must stop, she knew. I'm being sentimental. At least, though, she hadn't given them names.

A non-archosaurian presence prickled her consciousness and Elsa turned her head. Dr Dickhart was striding towards her through the tall grass of the meadow. He took off his hat and waved it at her.

"I know what I'm doing is wrong," Elsa said when he came abreast of her.

"What do you mean?"

"I'm treating them like pets," she said. "And they're not pets. They're weapons. I have to remember that."

"They are so beautiful," Dr. Dickhart said.

"I have found, though, that if you bond with them, they are more loyal to you, like any animal. And here we've created these creatures, won their trust, only to send them to the slaughter."

"They won't all go," Dr. Dickhart reminded her. "Most of them will stay here for research. Only the ones we've trained for the military will go."

"I find myself hoping they'll be too impractical after all to be of use. But then that would defeat the whole purpose of Camp Mesozoic."

"Come, let's go for a ride!" Dr. Dickhart said.

"What? Now?"

"Why not?"

"It's nearly dark."

"Nonsense, we've hours."

"But –" It didn't seem quite appropriate somehow; too celebratory just when they all needed to steel themselves to the fact that innocent golden days were over. But perhaps one last ride was just what she needed, a final burst of joy in the face of war, a warm memory to hold onto during the dark days ahead.

"Come," Dr. Dickhart was saying, "let's saddle up."

A short while later they were riding into the sunset, just like the end of a Western movie. America, Elsa thought, was so much like a movie, everything was possible, everything was big. Huge! The very landscape around them now stretched unbroken to the horizon. It was a land of extremes, of withering heat and deathly cold, of wealth untold and shocking squalor, an endless bounty of food and consistently lousy coffee. A country that was curiously forgiving of just about anything as long as you served that country effectively. The old Elsa Wild had disappeared here, disappeared into the heat and haze of Florida – whoever would have thought it? – she, this Teutonic product of Kaiser Wilhelm University. But she was American nonetheless. That, she thought, was the miracle of America.

And now she was riding like a cowboy with another foreigner at her side. What a country!

"Come on!" Dr. Dickhart called. "I'll race you."

And they nudged their therizinosaurs into a run, going like the wind through the balmy air, the dinosaurs carrying them up and down the slopes with no extra effort. The animals seemed to enjoy the run as much as their riders, taking pleasure in their speed and elasticity, almost as if knowing they were freed from the fossils that had held them for millions of years.

It was nearly dark when they dismounted on the high mounting blocks and led the therizinosaurs into the tack barn (Building #24). Elsa gently pulled down her therizinosaur's head with the reins to remove the bridle and bit.

"Dr. Wild," Dr. Dickhart said, helping Elsa with the reins, "would you like to have dinner sometime? We could drive into Kissimmee, there's a little tavern there, nothing fancy –"

"I would like that very much, Dr. Dickhart," she replied, smiling.

"Oh please, call me Alfred," he said.

"Alright… Alfred. And you may call me Elsa."

"Well then… one night this week?"

"Yes. I'll look forward to it."

Smiling, Dr. Wild and Dr. Dickhart continued to remove their therizinosaurs' saddles.

CHAPTER V

Schravenbach Castle, Black Forest, Germany,
winter 1942

The guards remembered the last time a shining, black, Maybach Zeppelin had approached their gates, remembered how all six cars had slunk out again with the bloodied, bullet-riddled corpses in their back seats. It was their duty and training to hold their superiors in awe and yet the guards on the ramparts, the guards at the gate, couldn't help but marvel at the death wish of this new set of men.

The guards above couldn't see into the car but those on the ground felt a mixture of horror and excitement when they beheld their SS *Reichsführer* in the front seat. The two men in the back they didn't immediately recognize, one in a general army officer's uniform, the other in a long coat with a great fur collar. The latter wore the armband of the Organization Todt.

There had been no warning of their coming. But the head of the SS needed no permission so the guards pulled the gates open and stood at attention as the sleek black car glided through. Loyal, awed, the guards banished from their minds what kind of condition *Reichsführer* Himmler might be in on the way out.

The car crawled over the cobbled courtyard to the narrow second gate. Without a word, without a command, the portcullis was drawn up, metal grinding and shrieking, the doors behind groaning open and the car slid through this mouth to the inner courtyard.

The driver of the car briskly got out and opened the passenger door for Heinrich Himmler first, standing rigidly at attention as the bespectacled little man emerged.

The *Reichsführer* coolly surveyed his surroundings, the thick, ugly castle, the black silhouettes of SS guards on the ramparts high above. He was excited but tried not to show it.

Behind him, the driver opened the back door of the car for Colonel Schumann who was followed out by *Reichsminister* Speer. Together, Himmler led the way to the iron-studded door, clicking confidently over the cobbles.

"Commandant Himmler...! Gentlemen!" the bug-eyed, befuddled doorman stammered. "This is an unexpected honor. ...Heil Hitler!"

"Heil Hitler," Himmler replied coldly. "We have received intelligence that Dr. Rot is to reanimate the tyrannosaur today."

"We are not too late?" said Speer.

"N-no..." the doorman said. "Is Dr. Rot expecting you?"

"No," Himmler said. "Step aside."

He pushed past the ineffectual little doorman and opened the door.

Inside the great hall, no beams of light filtered from the window on this cloudy winter's day. Himmler and his cohorts clomped over the floorboards as the flustered doorman pulled the door shut and hurried after them.

"Gentlemen," he cried, "I am afraid I cannot allow this."

"We are here to inspect the progress that Dr. Rot has made," Himmler said, striding forward. "She is using the valuable resources of the Third Reich and today she will prove to us they have not been wasted."

"But it is not safe, Commandant."

Himmler abruptly stopped and turned sharply to the doorman.

"Has the woman taught the beast how to use a machine gun?" he demanded.

"I – n-no –"

"Then take us to it," said Himmler, "the tyrannosaur, we are here to see it."

"I can't, Commandant!"

"Then we will go ourselves." Himmler pushed the doorman aside. "I know the laboratory is this way."

Himmler resumed his march to the far door and flung it open.

He paused for only a moment. But he was the *Reichsfuhrer*, a man who did not know fear – or wasn't supposed to – so he marched forward, past the wall where the demented design of bullet holes speckled the plaster, past the table and the floor that were still stained with blood. So much blood. Even seven years later it looked sticky and wet, like the rampage had just happened. The Nazi flag drooped there, collapsed down to one nail, hanging like a big black and red hanky on the wall.

But the doorman remembered that day. Illogically, he thought that if there were foreboding music, it would start about now. And as Commandant Himmler barreled through the exhibition hall with its disaster that no one wanted to touch, followed by the two Reich ministers, the doorman imagined the music increasing in volume.

And when Himmler turned in to the enormous, arched corridor, the music would switch key to A flat minor, a scale of seven flats ascending higher and higher with each step Heinrich Himmler took down the dark hall, the very tunnel from which that thing – Gretl – had emerged. The doorman watched impotently as Colonel Speer followed, following his *Reichsfuhrer* into the black, and then Colonel Schumann, neatly following one after the other.

"Gentlemen, I cannot allow this!" the doorman shrieked, edging along the wall to get ahead of them. "The situation is too unpredictable!"

"My understanding was that the tyrannosaur was controllable," Himmler said, marching rapidly. Death march music.

"Once it's trained, yes."

"You are not a scientist. Get out of my way."

"With all due respect, Commandant, you can't just enter the laboratory. You could disrupt the procedure."

"Dr. Rot is working for us, she works on our terms."

"Gentlemen!"

Himmler stopped.

"Is there something the woman wishes to conceal?" he said.

"Oh no, Commandant Himmler."

"Is this another covert scheme to disrupt the scientific advance of the Third Reich?"

"Of course not, Commandant."

"Then we shall proceed."

"Gentlemen," the doorman scurried after Himmler, "I have my orders."

They had reached the far end of the corridor where there was a heavy metal door. The doorman managed to fling his back against it, spreading his arms.

"I cannot allow it."

Deep, ominous thrumming, one note over and over as the lowly, inconsequential doorman from Rheinland-Pfalz stared into the face of the SS commander. Himmler had no eyes, just two gleaming circles of glass.

"Your name is?" he asked quietly.

"Schmidt, Commandant."

"Herr Schmidt," Himmler calmly pulled out his revolver, "you can let us pass by you or *step over* you. The choice is yours."

High, tremulous violins, suspense, the kind of music that came right before a gun shot.

"This way…" Schmidt said. He edged to the right where there was a narrow flight of stairs corkscrewing upward. "You can watch from the balcony."

The Reich ministers climbed up behind their guide, gradually moving up into the light. Schmidt was sick with dread but the others felt a mounting excitement. Halfway up the stairs they could already feel it, the electricity, heat, the air was crackling, the very air was excited, some unseen presence was roiling.

"It's magnificent!" Himmler cried, forgetting himself, seeing nothing yet knowing they were stepping into something... powerful. Monstrous. Deadly. It was intoxicating.

If there was foreboding music, it would be drowned out now by the noise. But that was intoxicating too, growing louder with each step, louder, LOUDER, until the steps beneath their feet vibrated, shook, *shook,* and all four men held onto the walls to maintain their footing.

Schmidt had to pause. Pushing through the crackling air and noise was like pushing through a wall. He had never witnessed *Dinolebhaftigkeit*, he did not want to now, it was too close to the gates of hell. The din and shaking pushed back on him like two strong hands as if to say, No! No further!

But then Schmidt felt the barrel of Himmler's revolver in his back. He would have let the men go on without him but there was no room to pass in the narrow stairwell. He forced himself on.

They stepped out onto the viewing balcony. And it was Hell.

There was nothing between the frail metal railing and the morass below. Every few moments there was a blast of light which dazzled the four men so that they couldn't see anything but they felt wave after wave of heat. The electricity in the air crackled around their faces, burrowed through their winter coats, took possession of their souls.

Their souls... they felt something – their souls? – being sucked from their bodies, their life, their essence, something in the monstrous laboratory was leeching on to it, drawing energy from it; they were at one with the thing being born below.

Speer cried out and clutched at his heart as if to keep his life within. Schumann cringed and clapped his hands over his ears. Schmidt fainted.

But Himmler stood. He felt the tendrils of something fingering through his body, time – a dead vault of the past – was cracking open. Heat turned to stone cold, it hit him like a wind and Himmler opened himself to it, lost himself in it, found himself unbuttoning his coat to take in more of it. A rush from very far away, visions of things he had never seen, no one had seen but only guessed at, were present now in his mind's eye and a new truth unspooled in his mind like a moving picture. Something was screaming, he was screaming, he was screaming with something, wind, something protesting dragged up from death.

He dared to open his eyes a moment and was at one with the glory of swirling flame and noise that was now a roar of – voices? Waves. Crashing waves and hollow voices. He was gone, was pure spirit, aflame, at one with fire and death and power, was all three, such a surge of power untold, he broke away from his body and felt a rush of sexual potency.

A flash of white light, pure white, pure life, that blasted through him, taking part of his spirit and searing it onto the wall behind.

Silence.

Himmler found that he had collapsed to his knees. Schmidt was facedown before him. Behind, Speer and Schumann had also slid to the floor and on the wall, permanently, were three burnt, black, silhouettes.

That smell... there was a new presence. It wasn't supposed to be there. Himmler, none of them, were supposed to be there with it. Himmler found himself soaked with sweat, no longer a flaming, sexual spirit. Below, he realized, was the new flaming spirit. He could hear it breathing.

And he was afraid. This *reichsleiter,* head of the dreaded *schutzstaffel,* architect of the *Reichssicherheitshauptant,* quaked in terror as that thing below breathed to life, as yet unseen – he was wrong, he should have listened to the little doorman, he would have run even now if his legs would obey him but they remained limp and useless, his whole body exhausted, as though half his life force had been drained.

He was a prisoner, he realized, helpless. He tired to crawl but his arms would barely support him. *Death!* No! Death was coming for him! Why had he allowed it? That woman – Rot – that ugly little woman! The bomb, they should have built the bomb, why hadn't he listened to Werther? Werther had seen this, Werther knew.

The heaving breaths drew closer, the heat of some living being was rising. Himmler started crying and tried to clamber over the prone Schmidt. He was vaguely aware Speer and Schumann were also moving feebly toward the stairs.

A *HISSSSSSSSS...!* A head longer than the balcony rose into view; Himmler looked right into the tiny, blazing eye. He was prey. His body reacted the only way it could. He peed.

CHAPTER VI

Camp Mesozoic, 1942 summer

Dr. Dickhart emerged from the little Camp Mesozoic post office, sifting through a few letters, a small package tucked under his arm. He traversed the narrow main street, passing the canteen, various outbuildings, laboratories, the small library, to a low dormitory-like structure (Building #16) and entered. Inside, he followed the linoleum-floored hallway to his modest rooms. He passed other doors, most closed, a few open from which quiet conversation could be heard. Dr. Dickhart unlocked his own door and entered.

Inside his spartan living room, Dr. Dickhart dropped his keys on the coffee table and immediately tore open the package, shaking out its contents.

A small shellac record. Dr. Dickhart ran his finger over the sleeve, tracing the words, "Franz Schubert, *lieder* from *Schwanengesang."* He took it to the record player on a small table in the corner, slipped the record out of its cover, and put it on the turntable. He switched the record player on and dramatic piano music began as Dr. Dickhart moved to the window and listened, hands held behind his back.

Then there was singing, a man's voice singing in German.

Loyal subject, the king is pleased.
A monster has come to the Black Forest.
Loyal subject, the threat remains
From the evil sorceress who betrayed us,
The evil sorceress who fled to the West –

There was a knock at the door which then immediately opened. Dr. Dickhart turned.

"I'm going to the archaeology lab," Dr. Gorman said. "You coming?"

"In a moment," Dickhart said. "You go ahead."

Gorman started to leave.

"What is that?" he said. "...German?"

"It's Schubert's lieder." Dickhart gazed serenely out the window.

"Leader?"

"Lieder." Dickhart turned to an uncomprehending Gorman. "A type of song, old German poems that Franz Schubert set to music."

"Uh-huh. ...Classical."

"Yes, classical." Dickhart turned back to the window. "My mother sent it to me. She knows I'm very fond of classical music. It's a new recording."

"Uh-huh. ...Well, I'm going, then."

"Yes, I'll be right along."

Gorman exited and closed the door.

Dr. Dickhart lifted the needle and placed it towards the beginning of the record, resuming his contemplative stance. The singing started again.

...the threat remains
From the evil sorceress who betrayed us,
The evil sorceress who fled to the West.
The messages you have sent were well received,
But now your mission is nearly finished.
Loyal subject, warrior for the king,
Kill the traitor, the wild sorceress.
Kill the wild sorceress.
Kill the wild sorceress.
The wild sorceress must die.
Your loyalty to the Fatherland will be well rewarded.
You have your final mission.

Then, a flat speaking voice.
This record will self-destruct in five seconds.

The final chords of dramatic piano music and the record blew-up in a small explosion. Bits of shellac pinged off the walls.

Dr. Dickhart was still gazing out the window but now with an eerie look on his face. He was transfigured.

"*Ja, mein Fuhrer!*" he said, quietly ecstatic.

*

"This wine's not bad," Alfred Dickhart said.

"No," Elsa agreed, "it's very good."

"You liked your steak?"

"Oh, yes."

In a modest tavern in Kissimmee, Elsa and Dr. Dickhart sat at a table for two, having finished dinner. A guttering candle flickered between them; the interior was dim. There were few other people. On the bar in the back a radio quietly played jazz music. Elsa wore an elegant white evening gown, her hair piled elaborately on her head.

"You wouldn't think of Florida as being a good place to get a steak," Dickhart was saying. "One forgets that this is cattle country."

"Yes, that's one reason we chose this location, there would be meat for the carnivores."

"Lovely climate, too."

"Florida is beautiful. After the war I think I shall continue to live here. I feel very safe here."

"It's a quiet place."

"It's more than that. I don't feel besieged by anyone, no one is forcing me to do anything. ...You don't know what it's like to work under threat of death."

"Germany must have been hell."

"No one took that ridiculous Hitler seriously at first. We all thought the madness would blow over in time. But now the Nazis have decimated every corner of German culture. The German sciences are headed by half-wits and fools. The world used to look to us as leaders in science."

"It will once again."

"Will it? So many people dead, or fled as I have. ...I have nightmares sometimes that the Nazis have sought me even here."

"Come now, you're being morbid."

"I'm sorry. Too much wine." Elsa smiled weakly. "It gives me too many thoughts. ...A funny thing happened today. Dr. Gorman actually had a short conversation with me, actually about something that didn't pertain to Camp Mesozoic."

"Yes?"

"He said you liked Schubert."

"Ah, yes."

"Your mother sent you another record."

"Yes, German lieder. I was listening to it before going to the archaeology lab this morning."

"I'm flattered that you're so fond of German music. Many times I've heard it coming from your room. Always lieder."

"Yes."

"Your mother must send them to you regularly."

"She does."

"By now you must have quite a collection. I would like to hear it sometime."

"Of course. Tomorrow perhaps. Come to my room, we'll have coffee. Now come, we should be off. We should head back before it gets too dark."

Dr. Dickhart and Elsa rose from the table.

It was dusk when they passed through the outskirts of Kissimmee and pitch dark by the time they drew near Camp Mesozoic. Dr. Dickhart drove slowly with only a small pool of light from the headlights to guide them. An occasional indistinguishable animal darted before the car.

At the entrance gate of Camp Mesozoic, Dr. Dickhart's ancient rattly Ford pulled up and was waved through. Shortly after, Dr. Dickhart and Elsa were slowly walking down the main street to the dormitory, greeting the night watchman who nodded and passed by sweeping his flashlight. There was no other human presence, the night belonged to the wild, the air was alive with cricket noise and unidentifiable calls of nocturnal creatures.

But there was silvery moonlight.

"Would you like to go for a walk?" Dr. Dickhart asked. "Let's visit the therizinosaurs."

"I don't think I can ride in this dress," Elsa said.

"A walk, not a ride. Come."

"Mosquitoes..." Elsa slapped her arm.

"Please? I love to see the dinosaurs in the moonlight."

"Well... alright."

When they had left the buildings of the camp behind them, there was the true feeling of being in another world. With rustles and sighs the trees seemed to communicate with each other. Just above, the air flickered with bats. The night was released from the grip of the humans, nature knew this and relaxed and basked in the peace.

Elsa wobbled through the tall grass in her impractical evening shoes, laughing. Still slapping at the mosquitoes, she was glad she had come, raised her face to the moon and let the night breeze – balmy and warm, like nothing in Europe – play with her hair.

A noise jarred the night and a moment later two headlights crested a rise before her. A pick-up truck slowly drove down the slope and Dr. Gorman glanced out the window as he passed, nonplussed to see Dr. Wild and Dr. Dickhart on what appeared to be a date. Elsa felt Gorman's eyes quickly glance down the length of her dress, a faint smudge of white in the dark. He drove by without a word.

Then Elsa reached the top of the slope and looked down on a scene from another epoch. The therizinosaurs drifted peaceably in the moonlight, reptilian silhouettes in the tall grass.

"Alfred, come see!" Elsa called. "They're so beautiful." She heard a click. "Alfred?" She turned. "Alfred!"

Behind her, Alfred was holding a revolver.

"Oh, how I have dreamed of this moment!" He leveled the gun at her forehead. "You -! You betrayer of the master race!"

"Alfred, what are you talking about?"

"I shall purge Germany's shame!"

"But you're English!"

"There are many of us in England who admire the Fuhrer." He came closer.

"I don't understand." Elsa backed away. "What are you? Are you from the SS?"

"I shall be richly rewarded by the Fatherland, a hero!"

"Alfred, shut-up. Put that gun down, you're being ridiculous."

Now Dr. Dickhart pressed the gun against Elsa's forehead.

"Is your killing of five SS commanders ridiculous?" he said.

"I'm sorry it was only five," Elsa replied, trembling. "...Go ahead, do it. I'm not afraid to die. I knew someone would come for me. My work is finished, anyway. The American program will carry on without me."

"A shame, really. You are a brave woman, a brilliant woman. Pure Aryan blood, a shame to waste it."

"This Aryan business is all nonsense and you know it. You are a man of science!"

"Yes. And science will prove the Aryan superiority. I have already been on expeditions to find evidence of the master race. Archaeology will prove that we have always ruled the world!"

"Then I am ashamed to be part of that race. Go on! Pull the trigger! What are you afraid of?"

There was a powerful gun blast and Elsa's face was splattered with blood. The world went dark. When Elsa opened her eyes she found herself still standing – alive – and Alfred still stood before her with a hole in his head. He fell forward like a tree trunk and Elsa reflexively stepped out of the way.

Behind him stood Gorman with a hunting rifle. He quickly moved to support Elsa whose legs now failed her and she half collapsed against him. They remained like that for some moments, the trees – disinterested – sighed and whispered around them.

"I'll help you get rid of the body," Gorman said.

There was no time to plan, no time to think, Gorman only knew that he had to take charge. Elsa was in shock. He heaved Dickhart's body into the back of the truck and then bundled a stunned Elsa into the cab. Gorman clambered in behind the wheel and started driving.

Elsa, nearly murdered, he thought as he weaved through the dark. It was too much to take in but Gorman had to make a decision. First decision: Elsa was alright. Dickhart was the bastard. Dickhart... that phony with his cricket scores and cheesy bonhomie! He knew everything, all of Camp Mesozoic's secrets. And Elsa, the woman Gorman had called Frau Dino behind her back, sat trembling and blood spattered beside him. He had heard what she said when death stared her in the face, she had not been afraid to die for truth. For America.

Second decision: where to dump the body.

"Where did you come from?" Elsa asked, staring unseeing through the windshield.

"What? Where did I – New Jersey," Gorman said idiotically.

"No, I mean –"

Gorman understood what she meant.

"I didn't know why you and Dickhart should be out in the dark, in that spot," he said. "So, I got out of the truck and came back. At night, with the dinosaurs, I always carry the rifle. It didn't make sense, you standing there in an evening dress. I didn't really think –" What had he thought? Had some sixth sense told him something was wrong?

"Thank you," Elsa said.

They were near the stream, they could smell the cattle carcasses. Gorman made a third decision.

He shut off the headlights as they rolled close to the reeking carcasses. The denuded ribcages were black in the moonlight. The tyrannosaur was active, its presence could be felt nearby.

"I'm going to need your help," Gorman said.

He jumped down from the cab and hurried to the flatbed of the truck. Seizing Dickhart by the feet, Gorman pulled him out and let the body drop to the ground.

Dubiously, Elsa joined him.

"I'll take the shoulders," Gorman said, "you take the feet."

"But –"

"Just do it." Maybe Gorman wasn't thinking clearly, maybe it was rage or disgust or a thirst for poetic justice, but he had made his decision.

Gorman took the shoulders, Elsa the feet, and they lugged the dead archaeologist as close as they dared to the stand of cypress trees. They were moving deeper and deeper into death, the tyrannosaur was unseen in the dark, they could hear its breath.

"We shouldn't go any further!" Elsa cried. "Leave him!"

"I don't want him out in the open, let's get him to the trees."

"*Robert!*"

The massive black shadow emerged from the trees, its yellow eye caught the moonlight.

"Quick!" Dr. Gorman yelled. "Throw him!"

Dr. Gorman and Elsa swung the corpse back and forth to gain some momentum and flung it as far as they could towards the approaching monster. Then they ran.

"Don't turn on the headlights," Elsa said breathlessly when they were inside the truck. "Don't attract it. ...Quickly, let's leave!"

"I want to make sure it gets him."

"No, Dr. Gorman!"

The tyrannosaur did not seem aware of the fresh meat, it was more interested in the unexpected appearance of the pick-up truck. It came closer... closer....

"Please, Dr. Gorman!" Elsa pleaded. "Don't be foolish!"

"Oh –" Dr. Gorman started the engine, his eyes still on the macabre scene before him. "I think it's going to – "

The tyrannosaur trod on the body, crunching it like a dead bug under its massive three-toed foot. Blood and guts spurted out.

*

The next morning, the tyrannosaur's handlers lured it a safe distance away. Near its lair, in the hot morning sun, Gorman, Elsa, and Colonel York stood in a semi-circle looking down.

"He was a spy," Gorman said flatly.

At their feet, Alfred Dickhart lay face down, completely flattened, lying spread-eagled in the middle of a giant tyrannosaur footprint.

"Oh, this is bad," Colonel York said. "This is real bad."

"He'd been with us a number of months," Gorman explained. "He was sending information to the Germans the whole time."

"Oh, lord…."

"It was only information on the day to day running of Camp Mesozoic," Elsa reassured him. "It had to have been. He had access to no other information."

Elsa, Gorman observed, had recovered herself from the night before, returned to her usual cool, elegant poise. Until last night, Gorman admitted, he had held this stance against her, thinking it a pose. But he had missed the real poseur in their midst. What he saw in Elsa Wild now was not a flimsily concealed agent of the Nazis but a strong, determined woman, a brilliant woman – fearless! – who had trained a tyrannosaur to mow down SS commanders and who, just last night, had helped him throw the saboteur to their own T. rex. Who was this goddess, this woman of steel?

"How can you be so sure," Colonel York was saying, "that Dickhart didn't have access to any other information?"

"I have already told you, only I possess the method of *Dinolebhaftigkeit*," Elsa answered him. "Believe me, he knew nothing. …He tried to get close to me, but he learned nothing."

A wave of nausea came over her remembering that this was the man she had enjoyed a steak with the night before. The dried blood at her feet and crusting guts didn't help.

"Still," the colonel was saying, "a Nazi spy, this is a bad security breach."

"They were very clever," said Elsa. "We believe now he received his communications from the Germans disguised in music."

"Music?"

"German lieder," Gorman explained.

"Huh?"

"Songs," Gorman said. "Songs in German."

"I overheard some of them myself," said Elsa. "They must have been coded messages."

"*Psh...!* The guy's blasting German music and that didn't send up any red flags?" Colonel York fulminated.

"The songs were always about dragons and – elves and forests, death and nightfall," Elsa explained. "That's what lieder is."

"You never questioned why anyone would listen to that crap?"

"He was English." Gorman shrugged.

"But a fascist nonetheless." Colonel York sighed heavily. "I'll take care of the body. I'll have to report this to the War Department. We'll try and trace his contacts. ...What'd you shoot him with?"

"I keep a hunting rifle in the truck," Gorman said.

"What's he doing out here, anyway? What'd you try to do? Feed him to the tyrannosaur?" Gorman and Elsa were sheepishly silent. "Bad time for this to be happening." The colonel turned away and the three walked back to the army Jeep. "Our country's besieged on all sides, and now from within."

"Neither Germany – nor Japan – will be able to sustain themselves through the war," Elsa said. "They don't have the resources."

"They don't show signs of flagging yet."

CHAPTER VII

Berlin, 1942, September

It was night. Colonel Speer had insisted on that. This night must be reminiscent of the greatest Nuremburg rallies. It would do the Fuhrer good. It was going to be huge, this debut, no one in Berlin had seen it yet, few outside the Black Forest had seen it. Colonel Schumann had seen it – *them* – and doubted the wisdom of parading the new weapons before the public in this manner, the weapons were untested, unpredictable. They were intended for battle, not display.

But Speer knew the Fuhrer, understood him, and parades of big things were just the thing to lift his spirits, stiffen his resolve, reanimate, as it were, the German people. All of Germany and the entire world would see the Aryan might this night, Speer had the camera crew in place.

So he was not worried as he sat near Adolf Hitler in the Fuhrer box – surrounded by SS guards – at the Olympiastadion. The air was cool but not cold, the sky clear, the field below a geometric grid of marching Hitler Youth, beautiful teenagers, girls and boys, the future of the Aryan race. A division of the Band of German Maidens, all in white, doing such a marvelous flag dance, black swastikas floating dreamily above their heads. The entire field was ringed three deep by boys holding torches, a ring of fire! So Wagnerian, Speer congratulated himself. And now the ring broke apart into hundreds of sparks, points of light in the dark as the boys ran onto the field and made swastika formations of fire. All up and down the field, rotating, flaming swastikas – you could see the reflection glittering in the Fuhrer's eyes – and those lovely girls sweeping the orange air with their flags. Speer himself was nearly moved to tears.

His teeth veritably vibrated from the loud, vigorous drumming that accompanied the spectacle. The primitive, gloriously barbaric noise escalated, the flags swirled into a frenzy, the flaming swastikas dispersed once more into flying sparks then reassembled at the center of the field to form the words, *Sieg heil!*

Speer stole a glance at Hitler. The Fuhrer was smiling.

The drumming concluded with one thunderous *BANG!...* and it was time. Speer rose and moved to the little forest of microphones at the front of the box.

"Citizens of Berlin!" His voice seemed to roar out to the ends of the earth, filling the bowl of the stadium and echoing up to the stars. "For the conclusion of tonight's Victory Rally we have a final exhibition, a tribute to the genius of German scientific superiority. Germany's most brilliant scientist, Dr. Griselda Rot, in conjunction with the Third Reich, is here tonight with Commandant Heinrich Himmler to unveil to the world a new scientific achievement, an achievement that displays to the world the forward momentum of the Aryan race! Behold!"

Albert Speer felt like a god, hearing his magnified voice as he gestured grandly – godlike – to the east gate of the stadium.

They were there, he could see enormous, black, lumpy shapes. The energy from them rippled ahead into the field as a murmur of wonder wafted from the audience. The huge spotlights mounted at the top of the stadium trained their brilliant white beams on the east gate, catching two bright points of orange. Eyes... their eyes, great black lumps with eyes, the moving lumps lumbering into the light. And suddenly it was fully there – Gretl, the colossal female tyrannosaurus rex, a creature of massive head, and legs like bridge supports, a tail as thick as a man, whose nightmare teeth hung down from a mouth as long as a car.

A collective scream went up from the crowd as this thing, tacked up like a nightmare jousting horse, entered the arena. Her head was covered in a chanfron, a steel mask for battle, the rondel in the center the size of a dinner plate, emblazoned with a bright red swastika. Segmented steel plates looped around the tyrannosaur's neck, the steel peytral protecting her chest and either side of the steel crupper over her hind quarters also bore huge swastikas. From underneath all this industrial barding hung a caparison, bright red cloth decorated with little black swastikas.

The thrill that Speer experienced as he beheld this nightmarish miracle of science, the flower of *Dinolebhaftigkeit,* was akin to a religious experience. What he saw was pure terror, controlled – yet barely. Unleashed, the tail alone would bring down buildings. For, most fearsome of all, what eclipsed the steel plates were the thick chains wound round and round the tyrannosaur's snout, thick and heavy like something salvaged from a factory's infrastructure. They looped crudely over the elegantly fitted chanfron, a testament to the dinosaur's barely contained wrath.

And atop this monster, perched in a saddle on the dinosaur's shoulders, was an incongruous little figure, a woman, her canary-colored hair glowing platinum under the spotlights. She wore a white lab coat and Nazi armband. Dr. Rot, triumphant. She clutched the heavy metal chain reins in both hands, pulling expertly on the steel bit the size of a tree trunk lodged in the corners of Gretl's mouth behind her teeth. Smiling, Dr. Rot rode her dinosaur onto the field to the screams of the Berliners.

Just behind her followed Fritz, the male tyrannosaur, just a little smaller, tacked up in the same manner. In a saddle on his shoulders sat Heinrich Himmler. He tried to ride with the nonchalance of an American cowboy but his military cap had slipped almost completely over his eyes and he dared not let go of the reins to straighten it.

The two monsters came shuddering across the field, each footstep shaking the grandstands. Many spectators quit their seats and climbed over one another to flee, clogging the aisles yet stopped and looked back, transfixed, aware they were witnessing a Second Coming, a true resurrection. It couldn't be, it was impossible! Yet it was there, snorting, shaking its head and clanking its body armor, its feet leaving deep, three-towed footprints in the turf. The Berliners stared, they fell silent, the tyrannosaurs were beautiful in their restrained violence. See what the Aryan race had done! Hope was reborn! Hope, in two armored dinosaurs who could snap any enemy tank in half! Screams turned to cheering, the cheering turned to euphoria, a collective, mass euphoria and the entire arena began chanting, *Heil Hitler! Heil Hitler! Seig heil!*

The German Maidens wildly waved their red and black swastika flags, the boys held their torches in one hand and extended the other towards the passing tyrannosaurs, yelling as one, *"Heil Hitler!"* An awed camera crew crouched in the shadows on the ground, filming Fritz and Gretl as they passed.

With a certain barbaric majesty, the tyrannosaurs were slowly turned towards the Fuhrer box. Speer backed away from the microphones, careful to project a sense of courtesy, not fear. He was aware of the other Nazi dignitaries in the box shifting nervously, every instinct telling them to flee at the approach of these two prehistoric monsters but they willed themselves to stay, eyeing the stony Fuhrer.

Spontaneously, the drumming began again, low, thrumming kettle drums to accompany the dinosaurs' slow, heavy footsteps, a drumbeat for every step that shook the stadium. It became an operatic moment, a work of art.

The tyrannosaurs were side by side now, coming closer and closer with each footstep to the Fuhrer box. The white spotlight followed them, magnifying every frightening detail of their slit nostrils, the ridges of their boney snouts that protruded from the chanfrons, the horrible reality of those thick chains that held death at bay. And the smell...

Colonel Schumann reached over and seized Speer's arm.

"No!" he said a little too loudly. "No closer! Please, the Fuhrer!"

The tyrannosaurs were too close and coming still closer. Dr. Rot and Commandant Himmler meant to ride them till their snouts touched the very edge of the box. Schumann started to rise, raised his hand to command them to stop when he caught sight of Hitler's face.

He had to look away. Speer had seen it too and had also averted his eyes, embarrassed. For Hitler's face could only be described as... orgasmic. His eyes bulged, his jaw was clenched in such concentrated excitement, in that moment the Fuhrer was so vividly aroused he looked like he might – like he could – right there in the box, at the center of the stadium.

And Dr. Rot and Himmler were drawing rein before him. Two huge tyrannosaur heads blocked out the light, two pairs of blazing orange eyes taking in the possible meal of measly little men before them.

Himmler finally reached up to adjust his hat.

Hitler, bug-eyed, on an ecstatic high, slowly rose and came to the microphones. The crowd quickly hushed and it became completely silent but for the tyrannosaurs' breathing. Some of the Nazi dignitaries behind Hitler put their hands up before their faces from fear and from the dinosaurs' strong odor.

"I declare this night, *Dinolebhaftigkeit nacht!*" Hitler bellowed.

The tyrannosaurs spooked slightly at the sudden noise, their armor and chains clanking, but Himmler and Dr. Rot pulled tightly on the reins.

"Tonight," Hitler bellowed on, "is the holy of holies, a night to be emblazoned forever in the annals of German history! Let this night be celebrated every year with feasting and music!" Ecstatic cheering from the crowds. "For tonight we have witnessed the pinnacle of Aryan genius! May the world tremble before us!" The tyrannosaurs exhibited more agitation, shifting and straining against their chains. Himmler and Dr. Rot pulled their reins tighter. "Let the world see the might of Germany! With all degenerate forces irradiated from the Fatherland, the pure Aryan is free at last to populate the world, to bring order and scientific advance to all!" More cheering. The tyrannosaurs tried to back away from the box. "You see today that Germany has done the impossible. We have raised the very dead!" Hitler pounded on the railing. "We have the power of the gods! Germany has the power of the gods!"

The tyrannosaurs, agitated by the noise, would not stand still. Strangled shrieks escaped through their muzzled jaws, they tried to move away but were barely contained by Himmler and Dr. Rot pulling on the reins. Hitler was arrogantly oblivious. Behind him the other Nazis looked anxiously at one another, some half rising from their seats in alarm.

Hitler was screaming.

"Germany has the power of the gods! Germany has the power of the gods!"

He gave the Nazi salute and the crowd cheered wildly. Himmler and Dr. Rot took this as a cue to leave Hitler's audience, turning their restless dinosaurs and retracing their triumphal progress across the field. Dr. Rot was waving again, her smile a little strained.

CHAPTER VIII

Camp Mesozoic 1942, autumn

"Yes, America, the Germans have done it, done the seemingly impossible, brought back to life a species of dinosaur extinct for millions of years," the news announcer intoned, accompanied by a tinny-sounding recording of Wagner's *Lohengrin. "What does this hold for the rest of the world? Where will the fearsome Hun stop?"*

In a darkened multipurpose room of the community building (Building #11) at Camp Mesozoic, Dr. Wild and Colonel York stood on either side of a flickering movie projector.

"What next from the corrupt and evil minds of the Nazis? Will they soon be able to raise the very dead?"

Dr. Wild and Colonel York watched the news footage of *Dinolebhaftigkeit nacht,* the two resurrected tyrannosaurs looking even more impossibly mythical on the black and white film. Gretl and Fritz's armor glowed silver and their eyes caught the light like two white-hot points of flame. The spotlights made the tyrannosaurs' great fangs gleam. The footage was generally jumpy from the dinosaurs' shuddering footsteps, giving the film a kind of delirious chaos, an ominous foretaste of what was to come on the battlefield.

Colonel York switched off the projector. Elsa looked very grim. They were silent a moment.

"Theaters have just started showing this newsreel all over the country," Colonel York finally said.

"I had read the papers," Elsa responded haltingly, "but I couldn't believe it to be true."

"Germany…" Colonel York said, "has *two* tyrannosaurs. One male. One female. Soon there's going to be twenty of them running around over there!"

"That's not what we really have to worry about."

"Oh no? I thought you were the only one who could do this, this Dino-leeb-kite thing, you swore to me you were!"

"Dr. Rot," Elsa murmured to herself. "… I underestimated her."

"Well that's just fine!" Colonel York hollered. "You turn this technology loose among a lot of maniacs in Germany and then swear no one could do anything with it! God knows how many other people, other countries, could start doing this. It – it boggles the mind what could happen."

"Yes… the abuse…."

"I mean, what next? Reanimated men? An army of walking zombies?"

"Possibly…" Elsa almost whispered. Then more firmly she said, "They might try it but I doubt it would work."

"I've heard that before."

"Humans have free will. I think even Dr. Rot understands this, otherwise she would have reanimated men from the start, not bothered with the dinosaurs."

"They'll reanimate the Kaiser…." Colonel York muttered.

"No, they want weapons. That's what this is about."

"Bismarck…"

"Colonel, they're interested in powerful weapons, not resurrecting German history."

"Sick people, the Nazis, they'll try anything."

"This is all bluff, really."

"*Bluff?*" the colonel barked. "Two flesh-and-blood breeding tyrannosaurs are *bluff?*"

"They're not sustainable! They have two tyrannosaurs, in time maybe a handful more. *We* have hundreds of therizinosaurs! Don't you see what they're doing? It's all for show."

"I don't know why I listen to you anymore. The therizinosaurs haven't been trained to attack a tyrannosaur. One look at a tyrannosaur and all our dinosaurs with all their training will run for the hills!"

"Colonel York, you know the number of cattle it takes to feed our tyrannosaurus rex to keep it satisfied so that it doesn't run amok. The more tyrannosaurs Germany has, the more resources it has to expend just to feed them. Soon they'll be stretched too thin and the whole effort will collapse. If you ask me, this problem will take care of itself. That's why I said it was all bluff, whether Germany realizes it or not. It looks good for the moment but it is completely unrealistic in the long run. Dr. Rot has no real understanding. She is pandering to the Nazis, there is no true scientific thought behind any of this. And if you ask me, what Dr. Rot did at the Olympiastadion was very foolish. Parading two predatory dinosaurs among all those people, it was very risky. But not surprising. It made a good show."

"I'll tell you one thing, Doctor, Camp Mesozoic's going to have a parade of its own."

"Here?"

"In Washington."

"What?"

"Right up Pennsylvania Avenue, past the White House, for all the world to see. No more secrecy, it's not necessary anymore. We're going to introduce our own technology to the world!"

"Oh, Colonel!" Elsa clasped her hands enthusiastically.

"Let Japan see it! And Germany! And not just the therizinosaurs but your camptosaur and – and that one on all fours –"

"The tenontosaur!"

"And those ostrich guys... they look like big chickens."

"Our ornithomimus."

"Let's show 'em what we can do!" He hesitated. "I guess there's no chance we could exhibit our T. rex?"

"*No.*"

"Don't you want to ride him?" Colonel York asked, smiling.

Elsa was indignant.

*

It was not logistically easy and everything had to be done in a hurry. Specially designed freight cars had to be procured, all kinds of permits executed, so many security clearances obtained. There was bedding for the dinosaurs, food, where to house them upon arrival in the capital.

The dinosaurs would arrive by train at the Washington Naval Yard and then march over the bridge to Anacostia Park in Maryland where corrals would be built on golf courses and open meadows. On the day of the parade, the therizinosaurs would be marched back across the river and up Pennsylvania Avenue to the White House. Roads must be closed, traffic diverted, news crews strategically placed, snipers discreetly positioned to pick off any saboteurs. And even before leaving Florida the therizinosaurs had to learn how to march in formation, the cavalrymen trained how to control them, adjustments made to saddles and uniforms.

A name had to be invented, different ideas were bandied about: Dinosaur Dragoons, Dinosauria Calvary... Theropod Infantry.... The mounted soldiers training with the therizinosaurs began calling themselves the Fossil Fusiliers. It was a joke, a name surely beneath the dignity of the brave infantrymen riding the therizinosaurs into battle, but the name stubbornly stuck.

Colonel York used the name in all seriousness when speaking of the unit, it was how the unit was referred to in meetings at the War Department. And when the Army reorganized the cavalry branch, converting from horses to therizinosaurs, the name became official.

Press releases announced the dinosaurs' imminent arrival in Washington and announcements of the parade. There was great excitement and increased preparation when word came from the White House that President Roosevelt himself would be there to inspect this new dinosaur division.

Then there was the mad rush to produce the uniforms. A shoulder patch was designed: circular, a red background, an image of the therizinosaur in black with a red eye, claws rampant. A motto: *The Past is Present.* Thousands of the newly designed M1942 McClellan saddles were ordered from the Jefferson QM Depot in Indiana, thousands of riding boots, specially designed tack for the therizinosaurs.

Dr. Wild and Dr. Gorman worked tirelessly together to organize the event, overseeing every detail, coordinating the needs of the military, the logistics of the parade, and the needs of the animals. They supervised the loading of the dinosaurs into their custom-built train cars, oversaw the shipping of the tack, procured the food, organized billeting for the infantrymen, arrived ahead of the train in Washington to make sure all was ready.

In the end, the animals largely took care of themselves, calmly tolerated the train ride north, adapted easily to the environment of the Maryland Park, fed contentedly on the different local flora. The infantrymen continued to drill them, practiced maneuvers up and down the gentle hills, familiarized the therizinosaurs with the local roads, much to the amazement of the local people. Some residents cheered as the soldiers rode by, some fainted, unable to absorb the fact that dinosaurs now walked among them.

On a crisp November morning, the Fossil Fusiliers made ready, uniforms donned, dinosaurs saddled. The "exhibition dinosaurs" (the ornithomimus, the camptosaur, etc.) were corralled or bridled as need be and marched out with their handlers ahead of the therizinosaurs. Crowds lined Pennsylvania Avenue, cheering, waving flags. Security was tight, police cars and ambulances were placed at regular intervals on the off chance a dinosaur would go rampaging. But the medics were only needed for those overcome by the sight of so many creatures raised from the dead.

On Pennsylvania Avenue, in front of the White House, Dr. Elsa Wild sat in a special viewing box draped in red, white, and blue bunting that had been set up for President Roosevelt and assorted VIPs. Sitting beside her, the president was in high spirits, grinning in anticipation and enjoying a cigar with the excitement of a boy waiting for the circus. Mrs. Roosevelt was there as well, wearing a lumpy tweed jacket with a great spray of violets and slightly lopsided hat. Vice President Wallace and Mrs. Wallace were seated just behind with Secretary of War Henry Stimson and Army Chief of Staff George Marshall.

Elsa graciously answered the barrage of eager questions from both the president and first lady. There had been some trepidation about the parade, Elsa was told. Would this exercise be a triumph of American know-how and grit? Or a total disaster with battalions of spooked dinosaurs running amok and slaughtering innocent Washingtonians for all the world to see? Humiliation or triumph?

"I taught a tyrannosaur to use a machine gun, Mr. President, I know how to control dinosaurs," Elsa assured him and went on to explain the docile flock-like mentality of the plant-eating therizinosaurs who were well under control by their riders.

They were coming. You could hear the cheers blocks away, coming louder and louder, closer and closer as the Fossil Fusiliers drew near. Ripples of anticipation went up and down Pennsylvania Avenue as the spectators on the bleachers murmured and craned their necks to catch the first glimpse.

And then they saw it. The tenontosaur, its blunt, potato-shaped head looming over that of its handler. Some people started screaming, some got up and ran but most stared with a mixture of fear and wonder. The handler was relaxed, the thick rope attached to the dinosaur's bridle was slack and the twenty-foot long reptile from the Cretaceous period ambled behind as though walking through a twentieth century American city was what it was born to do.

The U.S. Marine Band, ranged behind the viewing box on the White House lawn, came alive with a blast of triumphal brass. Slowly, the tenontasaur drew closer to the viewing box, looking about curiously, carrying its thirteen-hundred pounds lightly.

Then it came abreast of the presidential box. Roosevelt stared, Eleanor's hand flew to her chest and she gaped. Elsa smiled serenely as the military men behind her swore, then quickly apologized to the ladies. Mrs. Wilson gave a little squeak and the vice president swore as well in spite of himself.

As the tenontosaur passed, there was a brief squawking and undignified trombone sliding from the band as some members caught a glimpse of the Cretaceous period monster. But the band played on and there were no more gaffs when the camptosaur strode past. It was another ornithischian dinosaur, Elsa explained to the president, this one from the Late Jurassic period. It was a species that had been considered for combat, she said, but had not proved as efficient as the therizinosaurs.

The flock of ornithomimus was the last exhibition before the cavalry and they were the hit of the parade. Feathered and fluffy, blinking and twitching their little heads to take in these novel surroundings, they looked like ostriches with very long, pointy tails. Some children started tossing them popcorn and the ornithomimus charmed the crowd by catching the morsels in their beaks.

Tears streaked Eleanor Roosevelt's cheeks, so moved was she by this miracle of science. None of it seemed quite an earthly experience.

"Well done, Dr. Wild! Well done!" the president and other men in the box congratulated her even as Elsa explained that it was a team, not merely she, who had accomplished this scientific breakthrough. She began listing their names, wishing they could have been in the box with her, and then she pointed.

"There he is!" she cried. "Dr. Robert Gorman, our chief paleontologist!"

The crowd grew hushed again. They were coming, the new warriors in this war. They were heard before they were seen, the marching of hundreds of feet, a *one-two, one-two* step. The road and the bleachers began vibrating with it. President Roosevelt clutched his cigar more firmly in his teeth, Eleanor's hand moved to her chest again.

"There he is!" Elsa cried again.

Dr. Gorman, her colleague, her friend, her literal partner in crime, rode at the head of the entire division. For a moment, the world shrank down just to him, the thud of hundreds of dinosaur feet faded away, the viewing box and its important dignitaries dissolved. All Elsa could see was how handsome the dark eyed, dark-haired paleontologist looked in his loose-fitting jacket and trousers of army green, Cavalry hat and riding boots.

There was no insignia on his shirt and he carried no weapon. Elsa observed that his face was expressionless and he looked neither left nor right, not even acknowledging the viewing box. Elsa knew he was still ambivalent about the dinosaurs going to war.

Behind him rode the battalion's lieutenant colonel with the silver oak leaf on his shoulders. He also wore the loose, green jacket and trousers but had a pistol holster on his hip and the special leather saddle-scabbard for the .30cal M1 carbine over his mount's shoulder. Behind him, as far as the eye could see down Pennsylvania Avenue was troop after troop of mounted infantrymen and marching therizinosaurs, each troop led by its captain.

The long necks of the therizinosaurs arched gracefully, oddly reminiscent of a flock of flamingos. Their forearms and claws were curled at their sides rather in the manner of wings. The riders were seated about six feet above the ground and their mounts stretched to nine feet in length. Every man wore the loose green uniform and were armed with pistol and carbine.

The lieutenant colonel came abreast of the viewing box.

"*Pre-e-e*-SENT!" he bellowed.

Instantly the therizinosaurs presented their dreadful claws, three feet long, scythe-like, holding them rampant as they marched past in formation. Little cries of fear went up from the spectators again. No one tossed popcorn. Parents drew their children close. Even President Roosevelt pulled back a bit in his chair.

"Aren't they beautiful!" Elsa gushed.

One-two, one-two… the regiment marched steadily by, the mounted infantrymen saluting the viewing box. Roosevelt saluted back, the therizinosaurs a sea of scythes. The spectators were now silent, solemn. The celebratory music of the band seemed incongruous.

"Why isn't that man in uniform?" President Roosevelt asked, looking after Dr. Gorman.

"That's my colleague, Dr. Robert Gorman," Elsa said again, "the head paleontologist at Camp Mesozoic. It's largely he who oversees the care of the dinosaurs, who has learned their behaviors and works with them accordingly. It was he who has taught our men to ride them and handle them, designed the saddles and tack. But... he's not a man of war, Mr. President. The dinosaurs are his life's work. For them to be sent to the slaughter in war... the idea is unbearable for him."

One-two, one-two...

"The War Department funded your research," the president reminded her.

"Yes."

"And now the United States is at war."

"Yes, Mr. President."

"You were given asylum in this country because of your valuable scientific knowledge."

"And I am grateful, Mr. President. I don't want our dinosaurs to go into battle any more than Dr. Gorman and yet the team at Camp Mesozoic has trained them for just that, they've been bred for it. The therizinosaurs are ready, America is ready to take on the enemy, we all are ready – even Dr. Gorman will make the sacrifice for the greater good."

"So, he's the expert fella, yes?" Roosevelt asked.

"The expert – fellow, yes," Elsa said.

"This new division needs a major general. It looks like, in essence, this Gorman fella is the de facto leader already. I'll send the nomination to the senate for confirmation."

"Nomination...?"

"For Major General of the Fossil Fusiliers."

"Oh, Mr. President!" Elsa gasped.

"We're at war, Dr. Wild. It's time for Dr. Gorman to step up and do his duty. He's the only one qualified for the position. You said yourself he's ready to make the sacrifice for his country."

"Yes, Mr. President."

"Many of these animals will die." He nodded toward the marching, rampant-clawed division. "The soldiers, too. Many mothers are sacrificing their sons. That's war. And war can't be won without sacrifice."

"Dr. Gorman will do his duty, Mr. President," Elsa assured him. "He will consider it an honor."

One-two, one-two... the viewing box thrummed with the vibration, its occupants watching the troops march past. They could see the individual men's faces, the details of their uniforms, the ammunition pouches at their waists, the saddle bags. And on every shoulder, the division patch, a bright red circle with a black therizinosaur at the center, red-eyed, claws rampant and reaching out.

CHAPTER IX

Berlin, 1943, winter

Adolf Hitler threw down the newspaper upon his massive desk with a powerful w*hack,* his face twisted with disgust. Such an ugly old man, he sneered, that Roosevelt, with the dark circles around his eyes and those ridiculous little spectacles. The man was a cripple, anyone could see that. He wasn't fit to rule, weak, sickly, *old.* But then it stood to reason that such a pathetic specimen would rule over the American mongrel race. Yet Hitler was nearly apoplectic at the sight of the cool Aryan beauty at the president's side. Why wasn't she dead? He had been assured that Reich operatives in America would take care of it. And yet, there she stood like a movie star (disgusting, she should be married and breeding children for the future Reich) next to the fatuously grinning American president. Another man Hitler didn't recognize – serious, unsmiling, darkly handsome… Jewish? Wild's date? – stood on Roosevelt's left.

The article had mocked and derided the spindly little pygmy reptiles that comprised America's supposedly mighty battalion of battle-ready dinosaurs. One sweep of the tail of Germany's mighty tyrannosaur would vanquish the enemy's pathetic attempt at dinosaur military supremacy! The article assured its readers. Germany was safe! The article even included an illustration showing the size ratio of the tyrannosaur to the therizinosaur.

Still, Hitler didn't like it. No punishment was too severe for Aryan scientists who betrayed their race and defected to the enemy. And the newspaper also ran a picture of that infamous dinosaur parade, squadrons of marching therizinosaurs stretching the length of Pennsylvania Avenue, all those little heads and arched necks, claws rampant. Visions of sickle-clawed monsters raced through his brain; for a moment Berlin was overrun by hordes of therizinosaurs pouring down the boulevards like ants... and only two tyrannosaurs. He was right to have summoned the other scientist woman.

In the distance there was the sound of a door opening.

"Mein Fuhrer..." the SS guard's voice echoed across vast space. "The woman is here."

Hitler wearily glanced up. At the far end of his huge office the guard stood in a rigid Nazi salute. Hitler made a motion of acquiescence with his hand and the guard backed out through the door. A moment later a figure in a white lab coat stood tiny and inconsequential in the towering doorway topped with the German eagle.

Dr. Rot's eyes widened in amazement at what she saw. The room was reminiscent of the Olympiastadiom in size and grandeur. Her eyes didn't know what to take in first, the carpet that stretched to the corners like a flat sea, the eight floor-to-ceiling windows, the multi-colored marble on the walls glittering magically in the golden lamplight. Rare paintings and a huge tapestry gave the room an aura of a museum – or palace. But it was the dot in the farthest reaches of the vast space, a little mustachioed dot in the vague shape of a man that stood before a yawning fireplace under an enormous picture of Bismark, it was the dot that made Dr. Rot's bones turn to jelly, her blood run hot and cold, the presence of the dot that nearly made her faint.

But Dr. Rot rallied, squared her shoulders, straightened her spine and began her determined march across the cavern – which took on the quality of a silent film as her footsteps fell soundlessly into the thick carpet. Thus, she approached the little mustachioed god, silently, like a squat fairy drawn to the light.

It took almost a full minute to cross the room. The Fuhrer took on more and more detail, the hair plastered aslant across the forehead, the beetle-black eyes, the khaki uniform. It was... really him, *Herr Wolf*, Europe's Director. Dr. Rot hesitated and stopped a few feet short of him, unsure how close she should go.

Flustered, overwhelmed, she dropped into a deep bow.

"Oh – oh – your majesty!" Dr. Rot gasped.

"Fraulein," Hitler made a slight, indulgent smile, "welcome to the New Reich Chancellery."

"Oh – oh – mein Fuhrer, I am so deeply honored!"

"Come now, we have much to discuss."

"Oh yes, mein Fuhrer," Dr. Rot said, still doubled over. "I have exciting news!"

Hitler picked up the newspaper from the desk.

"Have you seen this disgusting photograph?" he asked.

"I – I –"

"Fraulein, please straighten up." Dr. Rot straightened and Hitler thrust the paper at her. "Here."

Dr. Rot took it and solemnly regarded the grinning threesome.

"Ohh..." Dr. Rot breathed, "the traitor!"

Hitler wandered to one of the great windows and looked out into the dark.

"The traitor has created an arsenal of dinosaurs," he said. "There was recently an exhibition in Washington."

"Yes... yes, I know. But mein Fuhrer, we have the tyrannosaurs."

"We have two."

"One would be enough to foil Dr. Wild's arsenal. One look at a predatory tyrannosaur and every one of those therizinosaurs will scatter!"

"Will they?" Hitler asked dubiously.

"It's their instinct," Dr. Rot insisted. "They're herbivores. The tyrannosaur is the thing to have. One tyrannosaur cancels out a hundred inferior dinosaurs."

"Yes…" Hitler turned back to the room. "This is why I summoned you to Berlin this evening. The German people must see you, must know that Germany is still at the forefront of scientific advance. *We* have the power, not the degenerate Americans!"

"Oh yes, mein Fuhrer!"

"Your laboratories will be moved to the capital. I will give you the zeppelin field outside Berlin."

"Oh, mein Fuhrer!"

"The people must see your creations, see our strength."

"Yes! Yes! …But mein Fuhrer, if we move the dinosaurs to Berlin, won't they be vulnerable to bombing?"

Hitler's face suddenly went purple.

"Berlin is not vulnerable!" he screamed wildly.

"Oh, no no no, mein Fuhrer, no no no…" Dr. Rot immediately dropped into a cowering bow again. "M-mein Fuhrer, I – I brought something for you. This is what I wanted to tell you, my exciting news."

Hesitantly, she backed away, still bowed, and made the long, awkward passage across the yawning room. She did not straighten up until she reached the inlaid double doors whereupon she seized the handles and threw them open. On the other side stood the bewildered SS guard holding reins of chain attached to a baby tyrannosaur. It was nearly as tall as he was. A special saddle was strapped around the dinosaur's middle and its flanks were cruelly branded with the swastika.

Dr. Rot took the chains, attached to a steel bridle around the dinosaur's head, and led the baby tyrannosaur into the room. Hitler looked on with a mixture of amazement and fear at the dinosaur coming towards him, chains clanking, floor shuddering.

Smiling, Dr. Rot led the baby across the sea of carpet as the creature peered about, birdlike, twitching its head right and left as though taking in the paintings on the walls. It made muted squawking noises through jaws clenched shut in a steel muzzle.

"Here, mein Fuhrer, for you!" Dr. Rot was beaming as she drew abreast of the chancellor of Germany. "They have hatched! The first tyrannosaur hatchlings in sixty million years!"

Awed... amazed... Hitler was rendered speechless.

"His name is Adolfi," Dr. Rot said. "He is yours, a gift from Schravenbach Castle."

"Fraulein – Dr. Rot –" the Fuhrer struggled for words, "I am astounded."

"Isn't he lovely? Just a few weeks old."

"You are a national hero!" Hitler was warming up for a rant. "A hero to the German people! You bring glory to the Aryan race! How many hatchlings are there?"

"Six, mein Fuhrer."

"How fast will they grow?"

"We're not sure, mein Fuhrer, but they're growing every day."

"Eight tyrannosaurs!" Hitler enthused. "And America has only one! A pity the hatchlings are not old enough for Stalingrad."

"We're training them already," Dr. Rot assured him.

"Look at those teeth!" Baby fangs hung from Adolfi's mouth. "Is he a ferocious little fellow?"

"He's been fed. As long as a tyrannosaur is full it won't attack."

Hitler moved to pat Adolfi's head and the dinosaur made to snap at him in a muzzled bite. Hitler jerked back.

"Oh," Dr. Rot laughed, "he's a feisty little one."

"That's how we want them," Hitler concurred, a little nervously.

"Mein Fuhrer, would you like a ride?"

Hitler would not like a ride. That saddled creature was a juvenile, yes, but it was still terrifying. But... he was Adolf Hitler, *Reich's Fuhrer! Herr Wolf!* Director of all Europe! What country did not bow in defeat before him? ...And yet, no tyrannosaur, baby or not, was going to bow before him but... that smiling little woman with the ridiculous bleach job, she was waiting. She worshiped him. She expected her Fuhrer to ride his tyrannosaur.

And so, Hitler ran a quick hand over his plastered bangs, straightened his jacket and approached Adolfi.

There was no stopping once the process was started and the Fuhrer had to conceal his anger at the awkwardness of his mount. He had to clamber up onto his desk – was the SS guard watching? – while Dr. Rot emitted encouragement and instructed him how to swing his leg over – no, no wait, wait, Adolfi, stand still! – that's it, mein Fuhrer, squeeze with your knees, gather the reins, now just give him a little kick –

And they were off with a leap!

It was nothing like riding a horse. The tyrannosaur ran in a leaping run, covering a third of the great study with each bound. They were headed straight for the wall when Hitler remembered to pull, *pull,* pull hard to turn the animal. Then they were bounding across the room again, heading straight for the fireplace and again Hitler *pulled* with all his might to avoid being hurled into it. He was vaguely aware of Dr. Rot laughing and clapping like a child, calling out encouragement and instructions he didn't hear. Circling around and around the room, the paintings and curtains passing in a blur, the Fuhrer gained in confidence, learning the feel of the ride, how to balance his body, how much strength it took to turn the dinosaur.

He kicked Adolfi a little more and the tyrannosaur switched to a flat-out run, the inlaid doors with the SS guard coming swiftly at him but he wouldn't stop! The guard flung the doors wide and stepped aside as the Fuhrer sprang into the great cabinet room beyond. Whooping, Hitler galloped round and round the twenty-foot table that was draped with a swastika-decorated cloth, round and round the twenty swastika-stamped chairs, the paintings and tapestries looted from Hapsburg palaces mere smears of color in the brilliant light of the chandelier.

More! More! He could ride forever! Abandoning all caution, he kicked Adolfi still harder, loving the speed, loving the danger, drunk on the power of controlling such a ferocious (baby) monster. Hitler throttled through the next door (hastily opened by more SS guards) and – oh, glory of glories! – pelted down the red marble hall.

He was the master! The tyrannosaur obeyed him! The walls around him were a speeding womb of glitter in golden light. He had done it! He had done it all! He had built this! The glory of Germany was his forever! He, the man from Braunau am Inn, and an extinct reptile, forever the symbol of his godlike immortality!

The festive jingling of the chain reins, the cowboy freedom – Hitler burst into song.

"*Deutschland, Deutschland über alles...!*" He turned Adolfi at the end of the hall and started back. "*Über alles in der Welt!*" Never was there a night such as this! The very monsters obeyed him! "*Wenn es stets zu Schutz und Tru-u-u-u-utze!*" Hitler realized he had never known true joy before. "*Brüderlich zusammen hält...*" Riding a dinosaur up and down a marble hall full of stolen art, "*Von der Maas bis an die Memel...*" The joy was almost more than he could bear, "*...von der Etsch bis an den Belt...*"

He plunged back into the enormous cabinet room, urged a tiring Adolfi around the huge table, "*Deutschland, Deutschland über alles!*" and thence to his study where he slowed to a trot at last and

74

approached the little woman in the lab coat before the fireplace. *"Über alles in der We-e-e-e-elt!"*

In the presence of the Fuhrer and the national anthem, Dr. Rot wasn't sure what to do with her hands, give the Nazi salute or –? Instead, Hitler clambered awkwardly off the tyrannosaur and onto his desk as Dr. Rot hovered and fluttered over him.

Hitler no longer cared if he looked clumsy before the SS guards. He was glowing. He was master, lord of all! Already visions of himself riding a fully grown Adolfi floated dreamily in his mind. He saw himself masterfully controlling the largest, most fearsome living Thunder Lizard in the world, holding reins of chain easily in one hand while he extended the other in the Nazi salute. Let the fat Winston Churchill see that and quake; and that sickly, shriveled American president. Hitler took great satisfaction that old Franklin wouldn't be able to sit upright in a tyrannosaur saddle.

Germany would have a triumphal dinosaur parade of their own – soon – surely. And he, the mighty Fuhrer, would lead it. Hitler's eyes glazed over as the walls of the New Reich Chancellery faded away and he saw himself riding a roaring Adolfi through the Brandenburg Gate on Unter den Linden… when the war was won….

There was a distinct *plop* followed by a reeking stench as Adolfi pooped on the carpet.

CHAPTER X

Bangloc Island, South Pacific, 1943

It was still night under the trees. The birds knew it was dawn and the first chirps were sounding. Private Hoshina, assigned patrol, moved carefully through the jungle. He knew they were out there – the enemy – but no one was sure where. Bangloc would be attacked – of that they were sure – but it was a question of when. The island was heavily fortified, gaps in the coral reefs mined, barbed wire spread over the beaches, the gun emplacements and bunkers on alert. They were ready.

Hoshina slid down the steep slope of jungle, wet earth, wet leaves, bird calls gaining in volume. At the jungle's edge he stopped and peered through his field glasses. Bangloc was safe. The barbed wire loomed darkly against the lightening sky... but it was wrong. He could see it was wrong but – it couldn't be. Great chunks of the barbed fence had been cut away, not just a few snipped wires but swaths several feet wide, cut cleanly and evenly.

The sun broke over the horizon. It was a nightmare. Huge three-toed footprints riddled the sand, a herd. Hoshina could plainly see where they had stepped into the soft sand at the waterline and then clustered together to slip through the gaps in the wire. So, it was true, the enemy was indeed using those prehistoric lizards as weapons. Hoshina had heard about a parade in Washington, it had seemed too outlandish to be real, or practical. But they were here!

Hoshina bolted back into the jungle and began a frantic scramble up the slope. How large were they? It was said a man could ride one. And that there were claws the size of scythes, sharp, deadly... that could slice through barbed wire. They were here! They had landed under cover of night!

Hoshina slipped, fell, staggered up, slipped again. What route had the enemy taken? Where in the jungle were they? They had spread out then, closing in on the island's defenses from different directions.

The ground started thudding. Not an audible thud but a thud Hoshina could feel. And an emerging presence, something large and numerous rapidly coming upon him. Swift, purposeful – there was breathing, panting – Hoshina dived into the underbrush, insects biting his face, and curled into a ball.

Heavy footsteps pounded past, so close they brushed the edges of Hoshina's hiding place. He could hear the great, three-toed feet squash into the mud, THUD-s*quash,* THUD-s*quash* as they ran past, lightly, easily, built for the tropics, carrying their burdens with no effort, the occasional s*wat/slash* as they macheted vegetation out of their way. One *squawked* in excitement, its rider sternly shushing it, as the herd stampeded effortlessly up the steep jungle slope. They kept coming, a waterfall in reverse, flowing ever upward to Hoshina's unsuspecting comrades.

He was honor-bound. Hoshina abruptly uncurled and leaped from the thicket, aimed his machine gun and – it loomed over him, blacker against the black trees through which stripes of light were beginning to pierce. The jungle was crowded with them, twinkling through the trees, flowing up and up, claws out, necks thrust forward, tails fully extended behind. It was terrifying, it was beautiful, it was awe inspiring. It was true! Hoshina stood paralyzed before the therizinosaur towering over him. The shock of it was its most powerful weapon of all.

The FF rider drew his pistol and fired.

*

Gunner Yokoyama saw their heads first, the bodies emerging so fast over the top of the ridge he didn't have time to understand what he was seeing. Claws... He screamed. Monsters! Awakened from the depths of the jungle, their sacred land defiled, they had come for revenge. They were coming directly for him. Yokoyama screamed again and fired his concealed field gun. The monsters fell like ordinary animals. There were men on the monsters' backs. They held pistols. They fired them even as their mounts toppled, the riders deftly rolling out of the saddles, getting to their feet, coming for him. Screaming. Who was screaming? Yokoyama could hardly tell over the roar of the gun. The men fell like ordinary men and now they lay still. Those heads again, alien, reptilian heads moving above the ridge, scythe-claws, pulling themselves over the ridge with them, charging at Yokoyama with claws spread. He mowed them down. Back and forth he machine-gunned the alien creatures. Who were those men? Were these the Americans? How many? Wave after wave of them, an inexhaustible herd.

One of them threw a grenade.

*

Even in the thick-walled confines of the pillbox, Gunners Nakagawa and Yoshida could feel the invasion. The energy of it rippled through the jungle, electrified the air. Then they heard the *rat-tattat* of the field guns. Peering through the gun port down to the beach they saw a similar scene as had Hoshina, chunks missing from the barbed wire. Looking more closely through their field glasses they too saw the beach riddled with strange, monster footprints.

There was a certain *shush-shush-shush* coming closer... and louder. *SHUSH-SHUSH-SHUSH-SHUSH,* the movement of a hundred feet climbing the slope under cover of jungle to the pillbox. Nakagawa and Yoshida seized onto their machine guns and fired at the trees. The *shushing* was disrupted, the enemy returned fire, bullets ricocheting off the concrete box. The little fortification held even as chunks blew off its steel reinforcements. In the brief pauses between barrages from the machine guns, Nakagawa and Yoshida could hear weird, alien cries, like huge birds, just below the tree line. Men were shouting – it was the Americans! But what? An enormous lizard broke through the trees. Nakagawa gawped, unable to take in what he was seeing. Yoshida was screaming at him, pointing his gun at the thing and the rider on his back. A second monster lizard emerged; its rider fired its carbine directly into the gun port, hitting Yoshida. He fell with a scream, bleeding. The first rider threw an object at the box but overshot it. Nakagawa fired upon him ferociously. The monster with the scythe claws fell just as the grenade hit the ground behind the pillbox and blew off the back chamber with such force Nakagawa was nearly forced through the gun port from the impact. Plaster rained down from the ceiling, chunks blasted into the chamber and into his back. Nakagawa suddenly couldn't hear. The unfathomable creatures were now pouring out of the trees, their riders shooting relentlessly into the box but as in a silent movie, a nightmare, a fever dream. Nakagawa fired purely on reflex. More and more monsters came, some fell as he returned fire, bullets shattered the broken wall behind him.

Another soldier on the back of a lizard monster had an object in his hand; his comrades covered him, a blinding assault of bullets, they hung on to their mounts with their knees while firing with their free hands, and the soldier threw the object. The grenade landed at Nakagawa's feet. He dived into the rubble of the back chamber and the pillbox exploded.

*

The whole island smelled of burning. Private
Ishiyama had left his post to creep to the edge of the
jungle and peered down to the beach. There he saw his
comrades marching in line along the water's edge at
gunpoint by the enemy. It was almost evening and the
smoky sun was slanting through the trees. Surely,
Ishiyama thought, his comrades would be shot. He
waited. At their moment of death, he too would die, die
with no stain upon his honor. He fingered the grenade at
his belt. But he saw the Amtracs coming and to his
amazement watched as his fellow soldiers were calmly
loaded in then taken away over the shallow waves to the
waiting warship. They would be taken aboard then, he
reasoned, and tortured and killed there.

He looked through his field glasses. His commanding
officers, standing together at gunpoint! Surrender...?
Impossible! He watched, waiting for enemy shots to ring
out, entertained vague visions of himself leaping into the
fray with an exploding grenade to save them from the
shame. But more Amtracs were coming and Ishiyama
watched in disbelief as his commanding officers were
herded onto them.

He was abandoned. They had forgotten him. Surely
they must have forgotten others, so scattered were they
and well concealed about the island. Had there been a
command to surrender? But that was impossible!

Something was coming. Ishiyama stiffened and
quickly scanned the trees through his field glasses. It
was coming closer, he could see a black shadow slipping
through the vegetation, made indistinct in the smoky
haze. As it drew ever nearer, the ground began to vibrate
with its approach. ...The enemy? A lost water buffalo?
A few yards away he saw it clearly as it stepped into a

beam of light, towering, a reptilian head, the long, arched neck, claws –

Terror and incomprehension galvanized him back up the slope towards his post and the field gun. A nightmare – hallucinating – the Americans must have sprayed something into the air, he was seeing monsters. But the thing was real, Ishiyama could hear it in pursuit, a man's voice was calling out sharply, gunshots were fired.

Ishiyama tripped, fell into the soggy undergrowth, rolled over and seized his pistol. He fired wildly, screaming, as the thing loomed over him. The soldier on the monster's back was hit and fell abruptly from the saddle. Dead? Ishiyama continued to pull the trigger but was out of bullets.

It shrieked – the monster – it raised its nightmare talons to strike. Ishiyama threw the pistol and it bounced off the thing's thick, muscled chest. A grenade would kill them both but Ishiyama wanted to live. In an instant, confronted with something he couldn't comprehend, the primal instinct to survive blew away every idea, philosophy, propaganda, *Senjinkun*... he scrambled to his feet and ran.

The gun, he must reach the field gun, then he would survive. He ran like a mad creature, prey pursued by predator, slipping in the jungle mud, that *thing* inches behind him, running effortlessly. The clearing was just ahead, the clump of bushes where Ishiyama's salvation lay.

For every ten steps he ran, the monster took two. It was on top of him as they both burst out of the jungle into the clearing. The bushes – the gun! Ishiyama's hands barely touched the leaves where his weapon was concealed when the dinosaur swept the bushes aside in one great slash, gun and all.

Ishiyama turned. He would confront it. He would die standing up. The claws came down.

*

Panting, the therizinosaur plodded back into the trees. Its claws were red. It found its wounded rider and stood over it, bloody claws rampant, in a defensive pose.

CHAPTER XI

Camp Mesozoic, Summer, 1944

I am coming for you…

Colonel York and Major General Gorman jounced along in the Jeep as Elsa drove. Gorman was briefing the colonel on the therizinosaur's prowess in the Pacific Theater, a fact known by this time to all Americans at large: the dinosaurs were perfectly adapted to the tropical climate and rugged terrain, resistant to disease, able to forage for their own food in the tropical vegetation; how they had carried heavy loads along the infamous Kokoda Trail, used their formidable claws as a machete, slicing their way through the dense jungle. They had proved adept at hand-to-hand combat, taking out great numbers of the enemy during fighting at close range in the jungles. Even in death, when they had littered the beaches alongside the fallen GIs, the therizinosaurs served a purpose, Gorman added, becoming a valuable shield against enemy fire in areas where there was little cover.

They had proven their mettle in battle. Their effectiveness as weapons was no longer up for debate. And now with the allied invasion of Europe and the liberation of France the therizinosaurs must be deployed to fight the tyrannosaurs said to be guarding Berlin.

I am coming for you…

Elsa wasn't listening to the conversation. She wasn't thinking about war and battles, she was thinking about the end. The very end. Because it would end. Berlin would fall, Hitler would be overthrown. The march across Europe was inexorable. The Third Reich would not fall without a fight and the fight would be fierce, Elsa knew. Her country – her former country – would be flattened. She could see the smoking ruins in her mind. She would never live there again. But she would go back one more time, with her dinosaurs, her creation. She and the therizinosaurs would be part of it, the destruction of an evil empire so that a fresh, better world could grow in its place.

And Dr. Rot. *I am coming for you.* Elsa was going to find Dr. Rot.

In the meantime, her therizinosaurs needed special training.

"It goes without saying," Colonel York said, "that Europe isn't the Pacific Theater. Berlin isn't Buna-Gona."

"It's new terrain with a different enemy," Gorman agreed.

"Tyrannosaurs..." the colonel said. "Intelligence says Hitler's got ten of them. At least ten. There's a breeding program."

"A tank can take out a tyrannosaur," Gorman pointed out.

"We're talking urban warfare. I foresee another Stalingrad. Shock groups, T. rex shock groups. It's gonna be block by block fighting, street by street, building by building. An armored T. rex can bust through any barricade, knock down any building, destroy any defense."

"Hitler's tyrannosaurs have never been battle-tested, Colonel. It's a lot of window dressing."

Colonel York grunted, unconvinced, as the Jeep lurched to the training site.

At last, Elsa drew up to the edge of a large, flat meadow. A unit of theriziosaurs were trotting about in the tall grass with riders on their backs, exercising. In the near distance was a slope.

"We are readying our therizinosaurs for the kind of warfare you speak of," Elsa said. "I hope this training exercise will reassure you."

Elsa stood up in the Jeep and waved her arm. At the signal, the riders continued their paces but with a certain heightened attention. In the distance someone blew a whistle.

Suddenly, a large effigy of a tyrannosaur was pushed into view from the other side of the hill. The therizinosaurs saw it and froze. For a moment, the world held its breath, the birds stopped chirping, even the grass seemed to stop breathing. It was the moment of truth. Would the therizinosaurs live up to their hard-earned reputation as fierce fighters or – they started shrieking and scattered in all directions, heedless of their mounted soldiers who tried to control them. The riders pulled on reins, calling out sternly but the therizinosaurs fled like a flock of frightened ostriches, their shrieks piercing the air, sending present-day birds flapping from the trees into the sky. Riders lost their balance and tumbled to the ground, calling uselessly to their mounts, dodging the onslaught of stampeding sauropods.

There was another whistle and the tyrannosaur effigy slid from view. Elsa remained standing up in the Jeep, staring at the empty meadow. The now distant shrieks drifted on the breeze. Gorman was at a loss for words and the colonel was disgruntled.

Elsa sat and put the Jeep into gear.

"They need a proper trigger to overcome their prey instinct," she said decisively, backing the Jeep from the meadow. "I know what to do. We will reconvene here tomorrow."

The following afternoon, Gorman, Colonel York, and Elsa were again in the Jeep at the meadow's edge. Once more the riders were exercising the therizinosaurs until there was the whistle signal. Abruptly, the Fossil Fusiliers turned their mounts to the hill and charged. It was a sight to behold, the therizinosaurs' necks and tails fully extended as they surged in one great herd on the attack.

Halfway up the hill, the tyrannosaurus effigy was pushed into view, this time with a swastika emblazoned on its chest. The therizinosaurs lunged forward at the sight of the symbol but then faltered, losing their nerve and scattering in complete disorder back down the slope. Some of the riders lost their balance, fell, and rolled down after them.

Colonel York covered his face with his hand.

"I'll have to ride with them," Gorman said, "I'll learn how to control the therizinosaurs with them, it will give me a better understanding of what to do. We'll try again tomorrow morning."

In the morning, Elsa sat alone in the Jeep with Colonel York. It was early, the day was still cool, the hot, thick heat that made the day tired and dusty was still hours away. The cool air and golden light lent an atmosphere of optimism as Major General Gorman, in the loose-fitting FF uniform, trotted amongst the therizinosaurs and their riders. He gesticulated to the men, his voice audible as he called out directions to control their mounts, urging them forward, directing them how to overcome the therizinosaurs' skittish behavior.

The tyrannosaur effigy, emblazoned with the swastika, stood in the center of the meadow. Fashioned from hemp, the monster leaned slightly, it had no eyes, giving it the appearance of a well-used, worn-out child's toy but made eerie with the black and red Nazi symbol. As unrealistic as it looked, it still frightened the therizinosaurs and they refused to attack it.

Elsa sighed with exasperation.

"They are animals, Colonel," she said before Colonel York could voice his disappointment. "They need to be desensitized. They are, after all, not guns you can just point and fire. They are living things that must learn."

Elsa advised her colleagues that the therizinosaurs be unsaddled and left to graze with the hemp tyrannosaur in their midst. They were trained to attack the swastika, they had only to overcome their instinctive fear.

So, the dinosaurs were left alone with their predator. They were not happy. They clumped together, they ran. One or two went a little mad and charged at the swastika, confused by their training to attack and their instinct to flee. Only hunger finally calmed them. A distance away, they began plucking at the grass. Small groups seemed to assign a lookout, one therizinosaur who would stand erect, eyes glued to the tyrannosaur, little head jerking this way and that looking for danger on all sides. The scientists of Camp Mesozoic observed with interest, they had never seen this behavior before.

The therizinosaurs grazed, they watched, they grazed some more. Hours passed. The sun rose higher. Elsa, Gorman, Colonel York and the other scientists grew drenched with sweat and faint from hunger – no one wanted to break for lunch – not wanting to miss what might happen next. Because it did look like something might happen.

Little by little the therizinosaurs drew nearer to the tyrannosaur effigy. They didn't like the swastika, raising their claws at the sight of it. They shrieked at it, hissed at the tyrannosaur, gained in confidence as the huge hemp thing did nothing. One brave soul gingerly prodded the effigy with its claws. Then gave it a little swipe. Inveterately curious, the others drew near. The tyrannosaur – the bully – was helpless. From the sidelines, Elsa and Colonel York watched with the other scientists, breathless, as the therizinosaurs crowded round, shrieking, hissing up at the monster, taking little cuts. Not running away.

Well into the afternoon, Elsa finally said, "I think they're ready for another exercise."

No one could wait till tomorrow. The riders saddled up their mounts, Gorman rode among them, and they urged the therizinosaurs forward.

This has to succeed, Elsa thought. It had to succeed for America, for the brave soldiers already fighting abroad. In this moment Elsa didn't care about science, about proving herself, she only wanted a weapon that worked. That, and she couldn't bear the disparagement of Colonel York if this failed.

The therizinosaurs, now somewhat desensitized, approached the hemp tyrannosaur cautiously, long claws forward. The riders prodded them with little kicks to their flanks, giving verbal commands, encouraging them to attack. Finally, one of the therizinosaurs slashed at the effigy. Then another therizinosaur, then another. Little by little the therizinosaurs crowded around, slashing, cutting, shrieking, one of the effigy's arms got lopped off. Gaining in confidence, losing their fear, the therizinosaurs attacked with abandon, the effigy rocked back and forth, it lost its other arm. Then, the leaning, eyeless, hemp tyrannosaur tipped sideways and thudded into the grass. In a frenzy, the therizinosaurs fell upon it in one shrieking, slashing mass. Their riders hollered encouragement.

The tyrannosaur effigy was no more, just a brown, tangled pile in the grass. The therizinosaurs nosed about it for some moments, lost interest, then wandered away, their riders stroking their necks and congratulating them. The scientists on the sidelines burst into cheers and applause. Threads of hemp floated on the breeze.

The next morning the therizinosaurs were further drilled in attack work. Back in the meadow, before the same hill, a new tyrannosaur effigy was pushed into view at the command of a whistle. This time the herd of therizinosaurs charged fearlessly to the top, attacked the tyrannosaur and shredded it within seconds.

In the afternoon, a third effigy was placed at the center of the meadow and the therizinosaurs, riderless, came running at it from all directions, surrounded it and shredded it.

"This is an enormous step forward!" Elsa exclaimed to Colonel York, who lounged beside her in the Jeep. "The therizinosaurs no longer need to be urged to attack. Their prey instinct has been overcome." She turned to Gorman in the back seat. "You have done excellent work with them, Robert." She smiled and added, "Major General."

"They are ready," Gorman said, looking pleased.

"Of course, all the tyrannosaurs in Berlin are made out of hemp," Colonel York said sarcastically.

In the late afternoon, the therizinosaurs were herded to the edge of the tyrannosaur's lair. A safe distance away, Colonel York peered through binoculars. His adrenaline was going as it always did in this part of Camp Mesozoic. There was that smell... rotten carcasses mixed with – what? Fear... death... tyrannosaurus rex. Beside him, Elsa was very still and quiet. He wouldn't let himself feel badly for her, this was war. It was necessary. Even more silent was Gorman in the back seat, a dark, still presence. Not long ago, Gorman wouldn't have allowed it, certainly would never have come to witness it but he was in charge of the division now. And America was at war. It was his job. So he sat, silent. Tense.

The bones of cattle were scattered everywhere. The therizinosaurs, minus their riders, slowly – but not timidly – advanced into the tyrannosaur's territory. They peered about, listening carefully. Then, the ground trembled.

In a stand of trees not far away, the tyrannosaur appeared. The FF riders, the scientists, all those gathered to witness the grisly experiment, watched in silence with grim expressions. The thunder lizard emerged from the trees, brilliant yellow eyes locked on this invading herd. It chose one and moved forward, rapidly, moving in for a swift kill. They would run, he would pursue and capture.

But they didn't run. Their claws came up. As a herd, they advanced towards the tyrannosaur, not running but moving lightly, closer... closer... they formed a circle around the tyrannosaur, closing in, already slashing the air threateningly with their claws.

Colonel York watched tensely through the binoculars. The tyrannosaur crouched low, hissed at the therizinosaurs who in turn hissed and shrieked aggressively. The tyrannosaur emitted a shrieking roar, and lunged at the therizinosaurs. A few shrieked in fear and ran but most remained, closing in.

Finally, the tyrannosaur attacked, seizing two therizinosaurs in his huge jaws, slicing them clean in half. The herd of therizinosaurs rushed in, slicing at the tyrannosaurus' flanks. The tyrannosaur slaughtered therizinosaur after therizinosaur, two and three at a time, but still the herd closed in. Even as the tyrannosaur killed the therizinosaurs with his teeth, the herd slashed at his head and neck. Soon the tyrannosaur was covered in blood, the therizinosaurs' claws were red. There was a great cacophony of piercing shrieks and crunching bones. Weakened by the assault from the therizinosaurs, the tyrannosaur staggered, attempted to retreat, but was surrounded. The therizinosaurs continued their attack, slashing. The tyrannosaur desperately tried to get away, trampling therizinosaurs, knocking over numbers of them with his tail. Weak from loss of blood, he faltered. Finally, he fell. The shrieking therizinosaurs crowded around, climbing on top of him, going in for the kill.

Slowly, they gradually moved away, splattered with blood. They wandered aimlessly around the dead tyrannosaur, exhausted.

In the Jeep, Elsa was white and stricken. She couldn't look at Gorman. Colonel York lowered his binoculars and sank back into his seat. Had Elsa glanced at him, she would have seen that the stolid military man was close to tears.

"It was a necessary sacrifice," he said quietly. "Now we know they're ready. They're ready for Europe."

The camp workers began moving towards the therizinosaurs to herd them back to the paddock.

"Let's take a look," Gorman said, tonelessly. "We need to assess injuries and how many have died."

When any living thing is attacked by a tyrannosaur, it doesn't survive. A therizinosaur either escaped the tyrannosaur's wrath or it didn't. Some, who had suffered a swat of the thick tail, lay stunned on the ground and were aided by the camp workers. Most of them managed to get to their feet and walk unsteadily off.

But the scene of carnage... Colonel York's steely façade failed him and he had to press a handkerchief to his mouth. As he picked his way through the carcasses, he couldn't comprehend how Dr. Wild could walk amongst then so coolly, and the major general, looking silently over it all, frowning. The reek of blood... severed therizinosaur torsos, the hind quarters found yards away. Dead therizinosaurs on their backs, beaks gaping, bloodied talons still raised in the air. Beautiful animals that just minutes before had run free, alive. Now, compelled by a war that was not theirs, urged by men they had trusted, they lay mutilated.

It was when the colonel stood by the slaughtered tyrannosaur that he lost control. He tried to make out that he was mopping perspiration from his face but he was really wiping tears.

"What a beautiful animal..." he said in a quavering voice. Unbidden, images of himself in peacetime, in a Jeep, giving dinosaur tours in a park like this, bravely exhibiting the tyrannosaurs rex, returned to his mind. It was a dream, the tyrannosaur, once alive and magnificent in all its terrifying glory had been a dream, an impossible dream. And they had killed the dream.

Even in death, Elsa was wary of getting too close to it. This was not Gretl of Schravenbach Castle.

"The carcass will be preserved," she said.

"You'll reanimate it?" the colonel asked.

"I can," Elsa said. "I don't know that I will. It is not necessary if the military has no need of it."

Gorman was conferring with the other paleontologists as to the behavior they had witnessed, how the bodies were to be disposed of. Elsa's mind seemed very far away.

"Are you alright, Dr. Wild?" Colonel York asked, somewhat regaining his composure.

"I'm going with them," she said.

"Going... where?"

"I'm going with them to Germany. I want to see Hitler's fall."

"You –" Colonel York exclaimed. "Germany! The frontlines are no place for a lady."

"Germany will fall," Elsa said.

"Germany may not fall," said the colonel.

"The invasion of France was the beginning of the end. I must return to Germany. I have unfinished business."

"It's a war zone!"

"And the dinosaurs are my creation. I'm going with them."

"Of what use could you possibly be? General Gorman will oversee them."

"I'm not going to be fighting any battles," Elsa told him. "I will follow behind with the therizinosaurs until we reach Berlin."

"It will be a military decision how the therizinosaurs are used."

"Europe is a different terrain than the South Pacific."

"Of course."

"The therizinosaurs will have to be used differently. They can't fight through the winter and I doubt America and the allies will reach Berlin before then. I estimate by this time next year – maybe sooner – if the campaign is successful, we will be at the gates of Berlin. That is where the therizinosaurs will fight, not before."

CHAPTER XII

Berlin, April 1945

The streets were eerily quiet and empty. Berlin was dying. The smashed windows of ruined buildings stared blindly over streets strewn with debris. Facades of elegant townhomes were pockmarked as if from disease. City squares were deserted, grand boulevards stood silent. Draped over the wreckage were enormous banners with German slogans written in bold gothic lettering with lots of exclamation points. Other banners depicted a fierce and vigorous Fuhrer.

It was spring. Spring came even to a shattered Berlin. It was spring in the ruinous New Chancellery garden where Adolfi, Hitler's pet tyrannosaurus, was being ridden around and around the smashed tea house by the soldier-servant in charge of his care. Adolfi was much larger now but still not full size. Into this scene Dr. Rot wobbled through on a bicycle, keeping to the garden paths, weaving around chunks of masonry. She cringed, fearing for her rubber tires as the paths glittered with broken glass from the shattered conservatory. The once manicured lawns were overgrown, uncut, sprouting weeds... ironically, wildflowers; wildflowers springing up robustly, almost shielding the debris of war that cluttered the garden, rather like the banners draped over the dead buildings of the city.

Dr. Rot, neat and tidy amid the chaos around her, bleached blond and white coated, peddled up to the entrance to Hitler's underground bunker and dropped her bike on the grass. Stopped briefly by the sentries at the entrance, she was then taken in.

She was led down a short flight of concrete steps, turned at a landing and descended deeper down another flight. The sentry opened a door and Dr. Rot passed through.

Inside the checkpoint antechamber, a sentry stood before an armor-plated door.

"Dr. Griselda Rot," she barked. "I must see the Fuhrer."

A familiar visitor, Dr. Rot was immediately taken through.

The large situation antechamber was luxuriously appointed, the walls hung with paintings of Italian landscapes, armchairs ranged along the wall on the right, an upholstered bench lined the left, and a huge table stood at the center. In the wall on the right was another armor-plated door before which stood another sentry.

"I must see the Fuhrer," Dr. Rot barked at him in turn. "I am Dr. Griselda Rot."

The sentry opened the door and ushered Dr. Rot through.

They crossed the small antechamber before Hitler's private rooms to one final door. The sentry opened it, stepped through into Hitler's private study and announced,

"Dr. Griselda Rot."

Dr. Rot entered, all smiles, but her face suddenly dropped. The study was also comfortably furnished, thickly carpeted, the sofas and armchairs covered in patterned silk. More paintings graced the walls, including one of Frederick the Great hanging over the desk. Adolf Hitler was huddled in an armchair, clutching his German shepherd puppy, Wolf. Hitler had aged shockingly, his hair gray, eye twitching, face deeply lined. He did not look up at Dr. Rot's entrance.

As the sentry exited, Dr. Rot rallied and put her smile back on. She moved to stand before Hitler.

"Mein Fuhrer!" She gave the Nazi salute.

Hitler, still not meeting her eye, gave a limp, half-hearted movement of his right arm.

"Mein Fuhrer! Extraordinary news!" Dr. Rot continued with pointed joviality. "Roosevelt is dead!"

"Yes, I know," Hitler muttered. "I was told this morning."

"Oh. ...But mein Fuhrer, now is the turning point. Now is the time of Germany's greatest glory. Our hour has come!"

Hitler stroked the puppy.

"Yes..." he said absently, "our greatest moment...."

"There! Gaze upon him!" Dr. Rot indicated the portrait of Frederick the Great. "You are King Frederick reincarnate! Berlin will triumph! At this, our most dire hour, with the Russians and the Americans at our very gates, Berlin will triumph with a spectacular victory!"

"Victory...." Hitler got teary-eyed.

"We have the tyrannosaurs," Dr. Rot barreled on. "Their time has come. I will prove worthy of your faith in me."

"Victory...." Hitler straightened, eyes fixed on the portrait.

"I will not flee Berlin, mein Fuhrer. Other rats may be jumping ship but I will stay with you to the bitter end – to victory!"

"Germany will triumph," Hitler said.

"Yes, mein Fuhrer!"

"The tyrannosaurs, our tyrannosaurs, will save us."

"And it is only the beginning. After we have won the war there will be more tyrannosaurs, more dinosaurs, a vast army! We will conquer the world, the Red Army pushed back to Moscow, the Americans running in retreat!"

Clutching the puppy, Hitler rose shakily from his seat and cried, "It is the miracle of the House of Brandenburg!"

*

Zerbst, Germany, 1945

It was night and Dr. Elsa Wild felt the wind in her hair as she rode in an open army Jeep. It was happening... it was happening! She wanted to relish every moment, remember every detail, the electric feeling in the air, the roar of the army tanks before her, the sound of the rushing water below. It was happening right now, triumph! She and her American cohorts were crossing the bridgehead over the River Elbe.

Ahead of her a column of army tanks was streaming over the bridge. Turning to look behind, Elsa saw the great herd of therizinosaurs following, mostly riderless but herded along by mounted handlers.

After crossing the bridgehead, the driver paused to get his bearings and Elsa stood up in the Jjeep to observe the scene.

"How does it feel to have crossed the Elbe?" Gorman asked her.

"Less than sixty miles that way lies Berlin." Elsa was brimming with excitement.

"We may move out as soon as tomorrow."

Elsa was exultant.

"I have waited ten years for this moment," she said.

"Come and see where we've been quartered."

Elsa sat down and the Jeep pulled away.

When they stopped again it was before a country manor house, gabled and vine-covered, old and elegant. All its windows were lit. Army Jeeps and an assortment of vehicles were parked on the drive and front lawn. Gorman's Jeep pulled up before the house.

"Oh, it's beautiful!" Elsa exclaimed.

Gorman jumped down from the Jeep.

"It beats an army tent," he agreed.

He went to Elsa's side of the Jeep and helped her down. Together they walked towards the open door of the great house.

The front hall was wood-paneled, a few pieces of silk upholstered furniture were against the walls which were hung with paintings. The hall – the whole house – was full of servicemen, hurrying about, loudly calling to one another. Some were engaged in taking a painting down and knocking it out of its frame. Elsa and Gorman walked into this hubbub.

They were met in the hall by an army sergeant with a clipboard. He saluted.

"Sergeant," Gorman said, saluting.

"Major General, sir!"

"Sergeant, this is Dr. Elsa Wild... scientist."

"Sergeant Bolton, ma'am." The young man extended his hand. "We're going to be putting some of your animals out back, there's a walled garden. Your rooms are upstairs, I'll show you."

The three mounted the grand staircase, passing two servicemen coming down. One carried a painting, the other a silver candelabra. Gorman and Elsa looked askance at them but the sergeant took no notice.

They traversed the length of an upstairs hallway, more jostling from servicemen, until finally at the end of the hall Sergeant Bolton opened a door.

The grand bedroom was large but cozy, an oasis of peace and beauty, softly lit by shaded lamps. There was a big, canopied bed, a mirrored vanity, and French windows leading to a balcony overlooking the back garden.

"Oh –!" Elsa exclaimed as she entered. "I feel like I'm in a movie!"

"I'm afraid yours is less fancy, ma'am," Sergeant Bolton said, leading her through.

He opened a door to a dressing room. Inside it was lined with cabinets and shelves, and there was a small daybed.

"Well, goodnight," the sergeant said, moving to leave. "Sleep well."

"Is there any word when we'll be moving out?" Elsa asked him. "Have you heard anything?"

"Not yet," Sergeant Bolton told her. "We're as eager as you. Goodnight."

"Goodnight, Sergeant."

The sergeant exited and closed the door.

Gorman glanced around the room.

"Pretty swank," he said. "Of course, you'll have this room, you're not sleeping in the closet."

"I don't mind where I sleep. I don't think I'll be sleeping much, anyway."

"I insist."

But Elsa wasn't listening. She went to the French windows and opened them. Upon swinging open the great, glass doors, the scent of damp earth and boxwood drifted in on a soft, cool breeze. The rather stuffily grand room became a different place, the outside came inside, pushing away the rules and norms of daytime; because this was nighttime, and the air was electric with hope.

It was also noisy with shrieking, reptilian cries.

"Oh, they're here!"

Elsa and Gorman stepped onto the balcony.

A large, walled garden lay below, its sculpted shrubs and silent fountains shadowed in the moonlight. The therizinosaurs were being herded through a wide, wrought-iron gateway and spread out quickly over the gravel pathways, nosing about, sampling the flowers, curiously stretching their arched necks. It was a scene that stirred Elsa's heart, the ancient, resurrected beasts flooding the nineteenth century pleasure garden. Let them play, she thought, let them rest and take their pleasure in this walled Elysium before diving into the blood and noise of battle.

"In just a few days," she said, "it could all be over. In just a few days Germany will be free from evil. Berlin will be liberated and we'll be a part of it!"

The excitement in the air was intoxicating. Even the dinosaurs felt it; they paced about almost agitatedly, trampling the flowerbeds and shrieking loudly. Gorman had always hated the fact that war had funded his research, his and Elsa's, but even he, now, standing on the very edge of victory, wanted to see it through, wanted his therizinosaurs to slaughter the enemy. What a triumph the Kissimmee Project had been, and not just work in an academic vacuum but work that was saving the world, literally saving civilization. His work... and her work. Elsa's... theirs together.

"Dr. Wild... Elsa," he finally said, "there's something – I've wanted to say, something for a long time, I should have said it long ago. What I'm saying is... what I've been wanting to tell you... that I owe you an apology. I said once – something pretty awful, what I accused you of. And I'm sorry. I was wrong about you."

"Thank you," Elsa replied quietly. "I am sure there were many others who thought the same as you. It's understandable."

There was something breaking between them, a wall that had been up for so long was finally breaking down. Elsa felt a rising warmth, an excitement that mixed with the swirling hope in the night air. In a moment, she knew, she would cross a threshold, and her colleague, this man she had worked with for years, would become something entirely new. They never would – never could – go back.

Before them lay the night and the soft breathing of the therizinosaurs. Behind them lay the bedroom with soft light... soft bed....

Gorman took Elsa in his arms. She looked up at him, her gray-blue eyes full of pleasant surprise, wonder, and Gorman kissed her.

They stood holding each other, Elsa resting her head on Dr. Gorman's chest.

"Less than sixty miles..." she said dreamily.

CHAPTER XIII

Institut der Biologische Erfindung, Berlin, April 1945

Within her private apartment, everything was vibrating. The paintings and gold gilt mirrors in the dining room rattled against the silk-hung walls, the Dresden china and silverware jingled on the mahogany table. The thick carpet did little to absorb the shockwaves that came right up through Dr. Rot's feet from the distant booming of artillery guns.

She and Heinrich Himmler were lunching at the table heaped high with chicken, butter, beef cutlets and bacon all spirited from Ukraine, plus liqueurs and champagne. The windows were open to the beautiful spring day.

Dr. Rot was drunk.

"- the Fuhrer's steward –" she laughed, "at the bunker, you know – " shrieking with laughter "–was hiding under the table, *HA!*"

Himmler morosely spooned up his soup to the rumbling of guns.

"Quite," he said.

"…the air raids…." Dr. Rot reminded him.

"Yes," the *reichsfuhrer* replied quietly.

"…doesn't have the stomach for it…."

"Yes."

"Oh, you know. …Oh… well… Blondi had puppies."

Distant thundering.

"I've seen them."

"Yes… the puppies. The Fuhrer is overjoyed."

"I know."

"Blondi… the Fuhrer's dog…."

"Yes. I know Blondi."

"I have *eight* tyrannosaurs."

"And that also makes the Fuhrer very happy."

"...save Berlin..."

"Indeed."

"...Save Berlin from the Russians. ...The Russians," she added solemnly, "will never take Berlin."

Booming guns.

"No," Himmler agreed quietly.

"Germany's finest hour... our greatest victory... I will never abandon the Fuhrer. 'My honor is loyalty!'"

"Heil Hitler." Himmler cut up his chicken.

Over the sounds of the distant guns came the nearer noise of truck engines.

"Oh, you're in luck." Dr. Rot got unsteadily to her feet. "The meat has arrived. Come and see! They're feeding the tyrannosaurs."

Himmler rose from the table.

Dr. Rot and the *reichsfuhrer* stepped through a pair of French doors onto a balcony. Below stretched a large, interior courtyard – cracked and weedy – where a convoy of trucks was pulling up, the first ones having already stopped, their cattle carcasses being unloaded. Men standing in the backs of the trucks threw carcasses onto the ground.

The surrounding massive neo-classical buildings had once been white. Now, Dr. Rot's *Institut der Biologische Erfindung* was almost black from the fires that plagued Berlin nightly. To the right of the courtyard was a huge hangar-like building where two men were sliding the great doors open. Even from where they stood a safe distance away, Dr. Rot and Himmler could hear the heavy breathing, feel the ponderous footsteps, then saw the great head emerge from the darkness into the light.

Himmler's flagging spirits immediately surged and a pleasant feeling of power warmed him. He had controlled that terrible beast, had ridden it through the Olympiastadion. He remembered that night with pleasure, the cheering crowds, the torchlight, an astounded Fuhrer. Watching the mighty creature come into the courtyard, the gleaming, yellow eyes, the dreadful teeth, grappling-hook claws and enormous hindquarters, he thought, Yes! The Fatherland still has fight left in it!

The first tyrannosaur was followed by five somewhat smaller ones, the rear brought up by the second adult tyrannosaur. They made straight for the meat. The trucks that were already empty quickly drove away, the men in the other trucks disgorging their carcasses as fast as they could for the approaching dinosaurs. The tyrannosaurs started to chomp and gobble the meat.

Himmler, surging with power, suddenly felt queasy at the sound of crunching bones and snapping tongues. The smell of fresh blood came to him on the breeze and he wanted to reach for his handkerchief. Dr. Rot, however, was smiling broadly and watching with hearty approval, though she swayed from too much champagne and had to grip the railing.

"Magnificent!" she said proudly. "Berlin's great hope!"

"And they are safe here." Himmler glanced at the surrounding buildings. "The walls were built very thick."

"Albert Speer... genius architect!" Dr. Rot swayed drunkenly. "And you... the great *Reichsfuhrer* genius! And I'm a genius. You... me... Aryan genius!"

There was a great clap of gunfire which rattled the windowpanes. Dr. Rot's hand flew to her chest, Himmler looked grim. In the courtyard, the dinosaurs raised their heads at the noise, paused in their feeding, listening.

Without a word, Dr. Rot turned and walked unsteadily back inside.

After pulling the French doors shut, the roar of guns was still audible but muffled. Listing towards the table, followed by Himmler, Dr. Rot seized the champagne bottle and poured it into her glass, slopping it over the sides. She collapsed heavily into her chair.

"I've been invited to the Fuhrer's birthday party!" she said after gulping half the glass.

"I'm not sure it will be much of a party," Himmler said, sitting also.

"Good food! Good friends!" She raised her bubbling flute to a great thundering of guns. "For all this we thank the Fuhrer!"

*

Zerbst, Germany, April, 1945

Flowers bloomed all about the manor house in the glorious spring sunshine. Soldiers lounged in the sun while others kicked around a ball. The air still tingled with anticipation as the Fossil Fusiliers and the rest of the American troops ached to move out and take Berlin.

In the walled garden, Gorman watched a little regretfully as the therizinosaurs were more interested in chomping spring leaves from fruit trees and gobbling daffodils than the hay their handlers spread about for them. Their necks arched elegantly as they stretched to see over the walls, shrieking and calling to one another, tearing vines from the walls and unconsciously trampling the budding flowerbeds beneath their feet.

Pitchfork in hand, Gorman helped spread the hay and did not immediately notice a preoccupied Elsa enter the garden. She came through the wrought-iron arch and stood looking at her magnificent beasts, the therizinosaurs feeling the excitement of the troops, as anxious to move out as the men were.

When Gorman did look up and catch sight of her, the world went quiet. Elsa... his Elsa. So beautiful. He had not known this kind of beauty before. It was not the kind of beauty that announced itself. It was a beauty that sneaked up on you, that welled forth like a spring. Beauty, that once you saw it, caught you forever, caught the heart, captured the spirit. How many years had he worked with her and not known this beauty?

Gorman had never been drawn to sirens, sex kittens, flirts, tight dresses and gobs of make-up. Women, generally, had not interested him. Women were theater. Women were bothersome, tiresome with their demands and subtle manipulations. It occurred to him... he really hadn't known too many women. He had been so absorbed in his work, women were distracting. Frankly, women were uninteresting. Dinosaurs, now, dinosaurs were fascinating. The thrill of an archaeological find, the identification of a fossil, that brought him alive. But Elsa... she literally brought the dead alive. Like a goddess! Dusty bones became flesh, she breathed life into everything. Had she not, in fact, manifested his very dreams? What man – what boy – had not dreamed of seeing real dinosaurs, longed to see them walk the earth again? And this woman – this Elsa – had done it. She was magic, she was witchery, he was bewitched, captivated. Caught. How he loved being caught. How he loved bowing before her, his goddess, this woman of unknowable prowess, who unlocked the secrets of the universe, created life like God Himself. Gorman was reminded of a quote from his distant Catholic upbringing, some saint... who was it? *Oh, I am ravished!*

He felt shy now in her presence.

"Hello!" Gorman called out rather stupidly, he thought.

Elsa didn't seem to hear him. He saw her sit heavily on a stone bench. Something was wrong and Gorman felt a terrible sinking sensation. She regretted last night, he thought. She was preparing to tell him, tell him it was all a mistake, tell him – that horrible phrase – they should just be friends. Of course he was not worthy of her, she was a loner, like him. Her work was her love. All this she would tell him, Gorman thought as he crossed the garden to her. He braced himself, there would be no histrionics, he would take a cheery tone with her.

"I think I'd make a good farmer," he said, brandishing the pitchfork. "This life suits me."

Still, Elsa didn't answer, only stared straight ahead. Maybe there would be histrionics after all.

"Shame about the tulips," Gorman barreled on as a therizinosaur chewed up a nearby flowerbed. "They seem to like them." There was no putting it off any longer. "Elsa...?" Gorman said gently. "What's wrong?" He sat next to her. "What is it?"

Elsa had tears in her eyes.

"I was speaking to General Simpson in the house," she said. "He just got back from headquarters at Wiesbaden. ...we're not going."

Wiesbaden... Simpson...

"General – what?" Gorman stammered. What did this have to do with last night, a night that still tingled in his body? Had they made too much noise, had someone reported them? "What do you mean?"

"They're leaving Berlin to the Russians," Elsa said flatly.

The war. Reality. Elsa was talking about the war. In his mind Gorman abruptly switched gears.

"What are you talking about?"

"The word came down from General Eisenhower," Elsa explained. "He believes the death toll will be too high. We're not moving out."

Gorman was silent.

"I don't understand," he finally said. Wasn't Elsa tingling with memory, too? Gorman didn't want to talk about the war, not just now, not surrounded by tulips and sunlight and grazing dinosaurs while sitting next to the woman who had shown him what it meant to be alive.

"I don't understand either," Elsa said bitterly "The Russians! They won't leave anything standing! Is this what it was all for? To come all this way, we developed the whole program as a weapon against Germany, and now! At the very hour! To just sit here –!"

The war. Yes. The matter at hand. As usual Elsa was far ahead of him. Now was not the time for doe eyes and sweet nothings. The war. They would talk about the war.

"At least," Gorman said, realigning his thoughts, "there won't be any bloodshed, for us. For them." He indicated the dinosaurs.

"I wanted to see them fight!" Elsa cried. "They were bred to kill Nazis!"

It was no use. He wanted her. He couldn't help it. How she thirsted for battle, the light of it blazed in her eyes. He would take her now, in the garden in front of all the therizinosaurs, in this primordial Eden, just the two of them, the only humans on Earth.

If only she would stop being such a Valkyrie, be like other women for just a moment, giggle and bridle, maybe angle for a marriage proposal, then Gorman would be able to pull himself together. But she wasn't like other women, she was like no one else, she lived for greater things, *Dinolebhaftigkeit*, taking Berlin, slaughtering Nazis.

"Elsa…!"

"They were in the Pacific Theater," Elsa was saying, heedless. "But it isn't finished! Just east of here lies the first cause, the evil that started this war, we're so close! And Dr. Rot! She's running loose!"

Gorman closed his eyes and pulled himself together.

"The Russians," he said, "will find her."

"But I know her, I know how her mind works, she knows the science of *Dinolebhaftigkeit*. The Russians won't know what they're dealing with." Elsa was almost hysterical. "I have to be there!"

"Elsa… Elsa…."

At last, Gorman put his arm around her. And he felt it, a melting. She had not forgotten last night after all.

She trusted him. They were still one. And as one they would fight the enemy. As one they would triumph. This would be their love, not diamond rings with a mortgage at the end of it all, but together, fighting evil, on the backs of therizinosaurs.

"Elsa! Listen to me!" Gorman said. "If it's the death toll General Eisenhower is afraid of he's thinking of the troops, not them." He looked again to the dinosaurs. "I wouldn't think there would be an objection to sending the therizinosaurs in."

"How?" Elsa demanded. "Alone?"

"Maybe something can be arranged. Even a – a collaboration."

"With the Russians? They're on the other side of Berlin."

"We have these weapons. Would they say no?"

Elsa considered this a moment.

"We will find a way," she said with decision. "I will be there for the fall of Berlin." She looked at Gorman, her eyes the same eyes he had seen last night – soft, passionate. "*We* will be there for the fall of Berlin. We will be there with our therizinosaurs, even if we have to go to General Eisenhower ourselves! I have to be there... Dr. Rot...."

*

Institut der Biologische Erfindung, **Berlin, April 20, 1945**

Dr. Rot was breakfasting in her dining room, her hair in a neat bun, lab coat snowy white, Nazi armband in place. The windows were open, curtains billowing in the breeze as Viennese waltzes played on a gramophone in the corner. Mingling with the music came the distant noise of aircraft, growing louder and closer, louder still, till it all but drowned out the music. Dr. Rot finally dropped her knife and fork and ran to the French windows on the balcony.

Looking up into the pristine, blue sky, a squadron of RAF bombers roared overhead. Dr. Rot craned her neck as they disappeared over the rooftops of the *Institut.* Shaken, she re-entered the dining room and walked slowly back to the table. The sound of the aircraft receded. It was almost silent but for the dreamy waltz music.

Suddenly, there were terrific explosions nearby. The shock, one after another, nearly knocked Dr. Rot off her feet as she grabbed the edge of her jiggling table where all the china and crystal were jumping and clinking with each explosion.

The air raid had begun.

*

The vast court before the entrance of the New Reich Chancellery was strewn with the debris of war, bits of masonry, exploded shell casings, shattered glass. Dr. Rot, wearing a pointed *Pickelhaube* helmet for protection, walked into this wreckage in the wake of the latest air raid. Stumbling and picking her way through, she slowly crossed the entire length, picking her way through this shattered Nazi might.

She reached the doors at last, guarded by SS soldiers, and was let through.

In the entrance hall, Dr. Rot passed between the pink and gray marble columns into the mosaic hall, the walls covered with enormous, heroic scenes, the center of the hall dominated by a huge German eagle. Dr. Rot crunched her way over broken glass. All was empty and desolate.

She proceeded to the massive marble staircase and mounted it slowly to the granite hall at the top. The roof, a glass copula, was shattered, all around were the brown and shriveled remains of once exotic plants, all dead now. The floor was strewn with broken glass and twisted metal.

Dr. Rot proceeded deeper and deeper into the eerily silent and empty Chancellery. She traversed the red marble gallery, 146 meters long with many smashed windows. There was more broken glass, so much shattered, glittering glass everywhere. Paintings that had once lined the opposite wall were mostly gone, the few that remained hung crookedly.

The Fuhrer's massive reception room... Dr. Rot passed beneath the huge, unlit chandeliers, a small figure approaching doors inlaid with rare woods, crossing over the enormous carpet that covered the entire expanse of floor.

SS guards opened the doors to Hitler's study. Far, far away at the end of the room, clustered around the fireplace, was a group of men in Nazi uniform.

Dr. Rot paused a moment and surveyed the scene. The room was dim, the heavy curtains hung closed over the windows. It was completely silent; if the men around the fireplace were talking, they were too distant to hear. A film of dust and dirt seemed to coat everything, making the once magnificent room appear dingy.

Gingerly, Dr. Rot began to cross the yawing, dark, sagging space. Had she really been here on that triumphant day just two years ago when she had presented the Fuhrer with the fruits of her labor, Adolfi? How happy the Fuhrer had been that day, joyful, riding Adolfi round and round this very room, delighted, galloping the young tyrannosaur through the reception room and up and down the marble hall. Dr. Rot sighed to remember.

Her footsteps made no sound on the thick, dirty carpet. She came abreast of the men at the fireplace and gave the Nazi salute.

"Heil Hitler!" she bellowed.

The men, distracted, had not heard her approach and startled violently, whirling around with frightened faces. Thinking for half a second that she was going to be shot, Dr. Rot reasoned that everyone's nerves were on edge from the air raids.

Seeing the little woman in the *Pickelhaube* helmet, they collectively let out a breath and returned the salute with an underwhelming, "Heil Hitler" in turn. Among the men assembled were Heinrich Himmler and Albert Speer.

"Well!" Dr. Rot said brightly. "Isn't this festive!"

"Indeed," Himmler said gravely.

"Such a fine day," Dr. Rot enthused. "Fuhrer weather!"

Yes," said Himmler. "Now that we're all assembled, shall we go and offer our birthday wishes?"

Everyone then moved towards one of the open French windows and exited into the garden. The ruinous chancellery garden was littered with debris. Dr. Rot, Himmler, Speer, and the other assembled Nazi bigwigs weaved around craters, twisted metal, and bits of unidentifiable stuff.

Far below their feet, the Director of Europe, the Wolf, the Fuhrer Adolf Hitler, slouched in his desk chair. Gray-haired, ill-looking, he sat alone in his study gazing with a mixture of mournfulness and hope at the portrait of Frederick the Great.

When his guests reached the situation anti-chamber, they found it still comfortably furnished with the paintings on the walls, but now cracks had appeared from the bombing. Around the table Dr. Rot, Himmler, Speer and the rest of the Nazi cabal gathered holding glasses of champagne. There was forced joviality and popping of corks. Then the armor-plated door opened and everyone snapped to.

For half a second, Dr. Rot felt that thrill that she always got in the presence of the Fuhrer but now... the thrill turned to dismay as a stooped Hitler shuffled in. It fell very quiet. Hitler's right hand was trembling, his left eye twitching. The assembled group gave the Nazi salute and a hearty, "Heil Hitler!" to which Hitler gave a half-hearted salute in response.

"Many happy returns, mein Fuhrer," Heinrich Himmler said.

"Our best wishes, mein Fuhrer," said Albert Speer.

"Happy Birthday, mein Fuhrer!" Dr. Rot said robustly.

The others concurred with more murmured wishes of many happy returns, etc.

Dr. Rot watched Hitler shuffle feebly about the room, shaking hands with his own trembling hand, smiling weakly. Then, without further ado, he forlornly shuffled out again, the SS guard closing the door behind him.

There was an awkward silence.

"Well," Dr. Rot finally said. "Isn't this festive!"

*

Torgau on the Elbe, April 25, 1945

The party was in full swing. In a banquet hall at the Soviet command post on the east side of the Elbe, a long table was draped in red cloth, well laden with food. A podium nearby was also draped in red cloth. The room was decorated with large pictures of Stalin and the Soviet flag, as well as smaller pictures of President Truman and rudimentary, stitched-together American flags. The hall was peopled with high-ranking Russian and American military officials, Russian women soldiers in new uniforms, and American journalists.

Soviet General Marshal Koniev stood to make a toast and everyone present raised their glass as well. They drank the free-flowing vodka.

Russian officers and Russian women soldiers sedately danced, mixed in with American journalists, both men and women, also dancing with each other and the Russians.

In a field outside Torgau, Elsa watched Major General Gorman ride a therizinosaur among the herd, giving directions to some newly mounted Russian soldiers, teaching. The mounted Russian soldiers rode about a little uncertainly.

Standing near a couple of army Jeeps a short distance away, Elsa and a group of Russian and American officers watched the therizinosaurs intently. Not knowing any Russian, Gorman taught by demonstration. Russian soldiers on the ground who had not yet mounted, stared in wonder at these otherworldly beasts. The river slid by a short distance away, churning through the broken girders of the destroyed bridge.

CHAPTER XIV

Berlin, April 30, 1945

Berlin was a skeleton. The four crewmen riding atop their self-propelled assault gun stared as they rolled through the suburbs. The hollowed-out apartment buildings were like dead faces, row upon row of dead faces, blown-out windows like dead eyes. Bricks, beams, ash had tumbled into the street like entrails. A civilian – a woman? a child? – darted like a frightened rat around a corner, the remaining civilians scattering through the smoke.

The crewmen roared past, following a column of Josef Stalin tanks, howitzers, trucks mounted with Katyusha rocket launchers and more open trucks full of soldiers. The center of Berlin was the goal but now the column slowed. Then stopped. For blocks behind, the invasion force ground to a halt, the roar of engines stilled to a muted, muttering growl.

Gunner Stepan Smirnov stood up and peered over the protective armored panels, straining to see why they had stopped. A barricade, he told his comrades. They sniggered. Flimsy tree trunks and overturned cars. They looked back at the might of the Red Army behind them and laughed outright. They waited for the tanks to push through.

Gunner Sergei Chalikashvili leaned over the other side of the mounted gun and saw heads tentatively poking up from behind the barricade, uniformed boys barely in their teens. The Volkssturm, Chalikashvili announced. Children! He and his comrades watched – almost amused – as shots from the boys' panzerfausts sailed ineffectually overhead.

Russian infantrymen shot at the barricade and the gunners watched as the Volkssturm boys were struck and fell, some dead on their backs in the street behind, others slumped forward on the barricade. Bits of the barricade were shattered when the tanks fired on it. The invading column began moving again and the crewmen's weapon rolled forward with it till they were close enough to see the Volkssturm's boyish faces beneath their huge helmets.

The gunners took cover again behind the gun's armored panels, spitting grit and ash from the eyes and mouths, black smoke making the air like evening. They hunkered down tighter as walls collapsed in clouds of dust, piles of bricks, but their hearts surged seeing the inexorable wall of Russian power behind them, the Red Army emerging like monsters from the fog.

Smirnov screamed. The moving gun stopped so abruptly it tipped forward slightly, throwing the gunners off balance. A truck of screaming soldiers crashed into them from behind. An enormous, armored tyrannosaur stepped out of a side street.

Smirnov stared, paralyzed. Behind him, Chalikashvili was screaming at him, Bobkov and Ritskoi were screaming at each other. The soldiers in the truck behind were bailing out, pointing their machine guns at the monster with a swastika emblazoned in steel. Bullets bounced off the armor like rubber, sparks showered down.

For Smirnov, things went quiet. It was a thing of beauty, the swaying red caparison so whimsically decorated with little black swastikas, the blazing yellow eyes, the gaping jaws coming lower, lower... someone was pounding him on the back. It couldn't be real! But the men were swinging the gun around and actually paused to watch in awe as the tyrannosaur dipped its head and took a *Na Ispug* "Terror Tank" in its teeth and, with a toss of its head, flung it down the street.

The gunners instinctively ducked and covered their heads as the deafening crash shook the air till their teeth chattered. *Go! Go! Fire!* someone was yelling. The gunners struggled up from their knees only to have a Matilda II tank sail over their heads. The gunners ducked again but Smirnov peeked over the edge of the armored panel, watching a nightmare unfold in real time, the tyrannosaur kicking Josef Stalin tanks onto their backs like toy cars. The monster trod down *Schnorfstrasse*, Smirnov could smell it now, smell it over the burning diesel, the dinosaur mashing entire trucks under its feet, crushing entire units of soldiers.

The foot was above him now, Smirnov saw it in all its crude, prehistoric glory, a three-towed claw, he was in its shadow, a kind of peace came over him, and then someone grabbed him by the collar and pulled him violently off the gun.

Bobkov pushed him into an alley between hollow buildings. Smirnov saw Ritskoi and Chalikashvili running ahead of him. He turned for a moment and saw the monster beast prowl past, shedding sparks from its armor, its tail bringing down rickety walls on dozens of infantrymen. Only then did he see the German soldier astride its shoulders.

From the alley, the gunners heard the sounds of crunching metal, gunshots, and collapsing walls progress down the street. Then all at once… it went quiet. Quickly, the gunners ran back to the scene of battle… and were shocked. Little fires burned around mashed vehicles. The street and sidewalks, the piles of bricks were running red with blood, wounded soldiers cried out and moaned. But the creature… where was it? A stricken howitzer crewmember, covered in dust and spattered with blood, recited in a daze that the tyrannosaur had disappeared up a side street.

Schnorfstrasse was completely blocked with fallen buildings, the Russians' ruined weapons and their dead. The invasion force had been stopped. There was dim cheering from the barricade.

Stunned, the four gunners watched officers try to rally the remnants of their units, artillerymen examined what was left of their weapons. Smirnov and his comrades stumbled over the rubble and edged around bodies to return to their gun. It had survived the stampede, only been pushed to the side of the street.

As they mounted their vehicle, the ground shook... then again... and again... exploding shells. No... more like... giant footsteps.

A second tyrannosaur burst out from between buildings on the opposite side of the street. A shriek of horrified disbelief went up from the survivors. Ritskoi jumped down from the gun and seized a machine gun from the dead hands of one of his fallen comrades, and began shooting at the thing. He screamed in rage as the bullets ricocheted off the dinosaur's armor, and watched impotently as the creature brought its foot down on a truck full of wounded soldiers.

But one bullet got the rider on its back. Wounded, the *Dino Kavallerie* rider pulled fiercely on the steel beam-bit in the corners of the tyrannosaur's mouth and urged her down a side street. The gunners fired at the monster's retreating back and a chunk of apartment building exploded in shell fire.

The wounded *Dino Kavallerie* rider rode between apartment buildings. Bleeding and barely able to stay in the saddle, he steered Gretl into a courtyard where other German soldiers were waiting. Two of the juvenile tyrannosaurs were also there, crouched in a corner of the cobbled yard. A female, Clara, and a male, Ludwig, were saddled, bridled with chains, half the size of their parents and waiting to be sent in on the second wave of attack.

Dr. Rot was there too in her white lab coat, *Pickelhaube* helmet, and *Kavallerie-Degen* saber strapped to her side. She waited tensely for news of the battle.

"Gretl, down!" Dr. Rot commanded upon seeing the tyrannosaur lumber into the courtyard.

Gretl lowered her great head to the ground where the wounded soldier half-fell from the saddle. A fresh soldier, *Dino Reiter* Zimmerman, was hoisted into it and rode back towards the battle.

Schnorfstrasse was a wreckage of over-turned tanks, assault guns, trucks, and dead soldiers. The Russians had been brought to a standstill. There was an attempt to retreat but the Red Army was backed-up on itself. There was no place to turn around. The four crewmen on the self-propelled gun were hunkered down behind the armored panels, catching glimpses of tanks cartwheeling past. They watched in dismay as tank after flipping tank crashed into buildings which then collapsed.

There were two tyrannosaurs. Smirnov stared, transfixed. The larger one was being hollered at by its rider – the monster had a name. ...*Gretl*? The scene became more macabre. Smirnov could actually hear the *Dino Kavallerie Reiter* shouting its name. But the rider was losing control of it – *her* – because Gretl was lowering her head to the barricade draped with dead Volkssturm boys.

"It's going to eat the children!" Smirnov cried to his comrades. The three others crowded forward to see and beheld instead Gretl prying loose a bullet-riddled Volkswagen. Raising herself to her full height with the car in her mouth, she swung her head and hurled the car into the air.

The second tyrannosaur was trampling through the chaotic thoroughfare. It looked up and immediately disappeared into a side street as the Volkswagen came flying through and landed with a spectacular crash upon the beleaguered Red Army.

The four gunners watched as a few tanks desperately managed to steer into the side streets amid the constant barrage of flying objects. A fat tree trunk came crashing down from the sky, part of a truck, great metal pipes, smashing everything in their fall. The self-propelled gun was wedged against a wall on one side and a crashed truck from behind. They couldn't move.

Gretl was then steered from the barricade and urged, stomping, up the thoroughfare. Seeing the armor-plated tyrannosaur bearing down on them, many Russian soldiers simply abandoned their tanks and trucks. They ran up the street, ducking into alleys and side streets if they could.

Bobkov started screaming wildly, flailing his arms. The other gunners tried to hold him back but Bobkov leaped off the gun and seized a machine gun from one of his fallen comrades dead on the ground. Bobkov turned and fired at the rampaging Gretl. He aimed at the center of the tyrannosaur's chanfron and the swastika emblazoned there; sparks poured off as the armor repelled the bullets. Gretl shrieked and reared up, Zimmerman skillfully hung on with his legs and fired back with his Maschinengewehr 30. Bobkov fell in a spray of gunfire.

Zimmerman then fired manically at anything that moved, shooting fleeing Russian soldiers in the back.

Dino Kavallerie Reiter Spitzmiller surveyed the wreckage of the Red Army from atop Fritz. The invasion force was decimated. The dinosaur beneath him was panting, probably hungry. Spitzmiller steered Fritz into a side street, leaving the wails of the wounded and intermittent crashes behind. The *Dino Reiter* urged Fritz over piles of debris and weaved through back alleys to the courtyard where Dr. Rot waited.

Riding into the courtyard, Spitzmiller saw German soldiers bringing in the dead bodies of Russian soldiers and unceremoniously dumping them in a heap. Dr. Rot scurried to Fritz' side and looked up expectantly.

"The Russian advance has been disrupted," Spitzmiller informed her.

Dr. Rot's eyes glowed.

"Excellent," she said. "Germany remains undefeated. Bring in the Russian dead! They are the tyrannosaurs' reward. Let them eat."

Spitzmiller dismounted. With the help of Dr. Rot and several soldiers, the steel beam was pulled from Fritz' maw. Fritz then nosed toward the mounting pile of Russians. Suddenly, it looked up.

Dr. Rot turned abruptly. Everyone in the courtyard froze. Clara and Ludwig lowered themselves into attack stance. In an alleyway off the courtyard – crouching there, claws poised – Dr. Rot screamed. ... Looming in the dark alley, claws raised, hissing... the American therizinosaurs.

More hissing came from a second alleyway. Therizinosaurs with rampant claws ominously inched forward. In the archway from the back alley... the therizinosaurs there spread their claws, eyes fierce.

Dr. Rot whimpered and helplessly backed away. But there was nowhere to go. The therizinosaurs moved in slowly but confidently, spreading over the cobblestone as the outnumbered Germans and tyrannosaurs contracted into a tight knot at the center. The *Dino Kavallerie* riders spun about, looking at this unexpected appearance with incomprehension.

"Fire!" Dr. Rot screamed. "Shoot! Shoot!"

The soldiers seized their revolvers and machine guns and started firing wildly. The therizinosaurs rushed in, shrieking. There was a deafening cacophony of shooting, screams, and roars. Some of the therizinosaurs were shot and they stumbled, wounded. Others took bullets repeatedly; they fell and died. But the onslaught continued, the therizinosaurs poured out of the alleyways, flooding the courtyard. The German soldiers were overwhelmed. The therizinosaurs, triggered by the swastikas, slashed the men to pieces.

A group of therizinosaurs moved in on the juvenile tyrannosaurus. Clara and Ludwig lunged at them with teeth and tail, knocking over numbers of them, biting, but with every lunge came a cut from a therizinosaur and the tyrannosaurs' snouts were soon streaked with blood. They had no riders to direct them and Clara was soon overwhelmed, biting and fighting to the end but overwhelmed by the flock of ripping therizinosaurs. She fell and disappeared under the herd. A mess of blood spurted and spattered the wall of the courtyard.

Ludwig bit and roared, pulling himself up to his full height as the therizinosaurs crowded him into a corner. He bit the head off one of them, throwing it over their heads where it landed with a *thwack* on the cobbles. The therizinosaurs shrieked and fell back for a second but then surged in again.

Dr. Rot heard noises she had never known before coming from the young tyrannosaur. It was screaming, and she saw it disappear under a crowd of vicious, slashing enemy dinosaurs.

The therizinosaurs turned, panting, their claws dripping red and trotted to the crowd that was closing in around Dr. Rot. Desperately, wildly, she swung her sword, screaming in terror. A forest of slashing claws, arching necks, and snapping beaks surrounded her. This was death, this was where she would die. *NO!* She sliced at the therizinosaurs nearest her, cutting them deeply with her sword, bumping into other German soldiers and tripping over dead bodies. The sword was sharp and heavy, the veteran of an earlier war, and Dr. Rot sliced off a beak, cut deeply into a head, another head. That one she stabbed in the throat, two more – three more! – she cut off their hands, the terrible claws falling lifeless to the ground.

In the seconds that the therizinosaurs fell back, Dr. Rot fought her way to Fritz who for just a moment stood unmolested as the therizinosaurs near him focused on turning Louisa into pulp. Just by swinging his bulk, Fritz was able to hold them off, knocking them over with a nudge of his huge leg and swipe of his tail.

Clumsily sheathing her sword, Dr. Rot grabbed hold of a dangling stirrup from Fritz' saddle and with great difficulty hauled herself up, clinging to the saddle as Fritz whirled around to face incoming therizinosaurs. Nearly losing her grip, Dr. Rot continued her awkward climb until she was at last in the saddle. With a practiced movement, she gathered up the reins and with a free hand unsheathed her sword. Kicking Fritz to get him to move forward she wielded her sword to her advantage from this high vantage point and slashed at the heads and necks of the therizinosaurs, all the while urging Fritz forward through the melee.

A Russian soldier mounted on a therizinosaur burst into the courtyard, urging on his mount with English commands. Another mounted Russian soldier emerged into the courtyard from the other alleyway, herding and commanding therizinosaurs before him.

Dr. Rot, screaming like a woman possessed, fighting like an ancient berserker, slashed and cut down therizinosaurs. She fought her way to one of the alleys and ducked into it.

Panting and gasping, Dr. Rot rode Fritz down the length of the alley, the tyrannosaur's bulk nearly filling the width. The far end of the alley opened onto *Stotzstrasse* where some of the invasion force was regrouping. She saw a Russian tank roar by. Abruptly reining Fritz in, she waited. Two more tanks rumbled past. She urged Fritz forward again.

Fritz cautiously peered from the alley. There were the sounds of Russian soldiers shouting to one another. Finally, Dr. Rot kicked her mount and Fritz charged from the alley, across the street and into the alley opposite. The Russians saw them and gave chase on foot, firing their guns.

The Russians pursued the tyrannosaur and woman in the *Pickelhaube* helmet down the alley. Fritz emerged into the next street, was steered left, then right around a corner and disappeared behind a building, the Russians still giving chase.

On *Schnorfstrasse*, Smirnov, Chalikashvili, and Ritskoi were pulling their gun around, watching in rage as Gretl still stomped about on tanks and trucks and soldiers. She mashed underfoot those already dead, coming closer and closer, nearly upon Bobkov who lay where he had fallen with the machine gun in his hands.

"Fire!" Smirnov screamed.

There was a loud boom. The shell hit Gretl's unprotected underside below her peytral and she exploded. The huge burst of blood, guts, and enormous internal organs smacked against the surrounding buildings, spattered down like rain on the crewmen. *Dino Kavallerie Reiter* Zimmerman was flung high, up, up, up, hung for a moment, then plunged, down, down, down, and landed with a lifeless *thud* behind the barricade.

When the fleshy debris had settled, there was a moment of silence. The self-propelled gun, the nearby tanks, the burned trucks, all were covered in a sticky film. The three surviving crewmen watched, stunned, as great rivulets of blood ran down the buildings in streams, brilliantly crimson against the dirt and dust.

A cheer went up from the Red Army.

*

In the courtyard, things had quieted. The German soldiers who hadn't escaped lay dead. Some dead and wounded therizinosaurs lay about among them. Russian soldiers tended to the pile of Russian dead meant for the tyrannosaurs. They carefully removed bodies one by one and lay them out in a line on the ground.

Elsa Wild rode into the courtyard mounted on a therizinosaur. Behind her on another therizinosaur was Major General Gorman. They wore the uniforms of the Fossil Fusiliers and were armed with revolvers and the carbines holstered on their mounts' shoulders.

They surveyed the grim scene, the wounded therizinosaurs lying on their sides in pools of blood, ribcages heaving. The Russian dead, the German dead in their slashed uniforms... Elsa couldn't look too closely. Her former countrymen, induced somehow, sucked into the madness that had consumed her country, her country that had once produced the greatest musicians, philosophers, poets and artists. Once, the world had looked to Germany as the leader in science. Now, the madness had reduced Germany to this, piles of dead men, wasted in the name of lies, who lay on the filthy ground as the great city of Berlin crumbled all around them, lay there with slashed faces, missing limbs... there was a head in the far corner of the courtyard.

Elsa stifled a wave of nausea – the smell of blood was overwhelming – and told herself not to think. Not now. Think later. Right now, tend to the wounded therizinosaurs. She jumped down from the saddle and moved to the nearest gasping, bleeding animal, kneeling beside it.

Gorman dismounted as well and came to her.

"Some of them will have to be put down," Elsa said.

"We'll save the ones that we can," said Gorman.

Elsa rose and glanced about, seeing the mashed remains of the juvenile tyrannosaurs. She went to one of them, finding its head still largely intact, its bloody ribs exposed. Leaning gingerly over the remains, she looked carefully at what was left of the tyrannosaur's flank.

"Major General!" she called. When Gorman joined her, she pointed to the remains. "She's been branded. See the swastika? And her name... Clara. She's the offspring of the breeding pair."

"Our intelligence says there are others at different parts of the city," Gorman said. "Lilli and Ricard are at Spandau, and Johannes is in the Tiergarten."

Elsa looked up at him.

"They were named," Gorman explained, "after famous German musicians."

Elsa turned back to Clara. The American therizinosaurs had done their job, excellent work, but... more waste.

She straightened up and looked over the courtyard.

"Dr. Rot must have been here," she said.

"Look among the dead," said Gorman, scanning the scattered bodies.

"Soldier!" Elsa called. A Russian soldier approached her. "Dr. Rot... Griselda Rot...."

Elsa switched to rudimentary Russian. The soldier understood and started describing the battle in Russian. He made slashing movements with his arm and pointed to the alley that Dr. Rot had escaped through. Elsa thanked him.

"She was here," Elsa told Gorman. "She got away. I gather she had one of the tyrannosaurs with her."

"Leave her to the Russians," Gorman advised. "Or she's probably headed west, she'll surrender to the Americans."

"Dr. Rot isn't likely to surrender to anybody. And if the Russians capture her, they may force her to work for them. I must find her."

She picked her way over the blood and around the dead towards her therizinosaur.

"Elsa," said Gorman, "where are you going?"

Elsa pulled the reins down to lower her mount.

"Dr. Rot on the back of a tyrannosaur can't be hard to find," she replied. "She won't have gotten far."

"You're going after her?" Gorman was incredulous.

"Give me a leg up."

"Alone? Elsa, the entire city is an active combat zone!"

"I think she'll gravitate to what's left of the center of power. I'll find her."

"Elsa!" He seized her and kissed her. They clung to each other a moment. Slowly, they parted.

"Give me a leg up," Elsa said gently.

Gorman helped her into the saddle and then watched as Elsa rode across the courtyard and disappeared into the alley.

CHAPTER XV

Vossstrasse, Berlin

Dr. Rot was slapping the side of Fritz to urge him faster along the *Vossstrasse*. The city was on fire. Buildings collapsed into the street all around her and it was only with a great deal of slapping and screaming that she forced the tyrannosaur over the piles of bricks, burning wood, and overturned cars in their way.

Her eyes teared from the smoke and she saw the burning world all around her as in a blurry dream, a nightmare replete with the black skeletons of trees, scattered dead bodies, vague figures drifting in and out of the smoke. And relentless, bone-shaking explosions.

Fritz was scared, shrieking, trying to duck into the relative safety of the alleys but Dr. Rot sawed mercilessly on the steel bit in the corners of his mouth. She slapped and cut his sides to make him go faster.

Gasping and coughing, Dr. Rot no longer knew the city, it had been burned and blown-up beyond recognition. Squinting into the smoke, she tried to find a familiar landmark, a shopfront, a lamppost, anything to orient herself.

A cloud of smoke drifted past on her left and out of the haze, Dr. Rot saw it. The New Reich Chancellery, riddled from flak, pockmarked like a diseased face, a hundred smashed windows like dead eyes. A dead building. A dead Berlin.

With no time to think of fitting symbols, Dr. Rot kicked Fritz over the debris of war and steered him into the chancellery garden.

The garden was no oasis, littered and gutted, but Dr. Rot knew succor was at hand. She had made it. She would be with her Fuhrer and all would be well. Yes, yes, it would be well.

Dr. Rot rode a panting Fritz to the entrance of Hitler's bunker. She pulled abruptly on the reins, however, and stopped, seeing something she didn't understand.

In a grassy but littered area near the entrance, Heinrich Himmler and a group of Nazi officials stood over a small fire on the ground, giving the Nazi salute.

"Down! ...Down! ...Down! Down!" Dr. Rot commanded Fritz.

Slowly, the tyrannosaur lowered itself and Dr. Rot slid out of the saddle, jumping to the ground.

Himmler continued saluting. Dr. Rot approached him from behind.

"Commandant! Commandant Himmler!" Dr. Rot hollered. The other men began to move away. "I must see the Fuhrer," Dr. Rot was babbling. "The Russians have therizinosaurs, hundreds of them. The tyrannosaurs disrupted the Russian advance and then all these therizinosaurs – the Americans, they must have got them from the Americans – I barely got away with my life, I've been riding the streets for hours, the Russians are everywhere but I had to see – oh –" Dr. Rot covered her nose at the smell from the fire. "What's that?"

Himmler slowly lowered his arm.

"Mein Fuhrer," he said.

Dr. Rot was incredulous, uncomprehending. Her hands flew to her face and she screamed, collapsing to her knees.

"*Oh...!*" she wailed. "Who did this? Who did this?"

"Suicide," Himmler said.

"No! *No!*" Dr. Rot cried. "I don't believe it! Why?"

Behind her, Fritz was lumbering towards them.

"It is finished for him," Himmler said. "It is now up to me to negotiate a peace with the allies."

Dr. Rot continued to sit on the ground, stunned.

"Negotiate..." Dr. Rot was dazed. "No, Berlin will not fall."

The fire had mostly burned itself out. Fritz lumbered up beside Dr. Rot and bent down to the burned body. He started to nibble at Hitler's charred feet.

"Fritz, no!" Dr. Rot swatted at his huge head. "Stop that!"

"Come with us," Himmler said. "A group of us are going to break out of Berlin through the U-Bahn tunnel."

"No! No!"

"It's your last chance."

"What about Fritz? The tyrannosaurs? My life's work!"

Himmler eyed the tyrannosaur with interest.

"Good at getting through the barricades, is he?" he said.

"...yes..." Dr. Rot gazed at the charred body.

"Down!" Himmler ordered Fritz. The tyrannosaur lowered himself. "The chancellery is being evacuated. Go with the others." He heaved himself into the saddle.

Dr. Rot whirled around.

"What are you doing?" she cried.

Himmler gathered up the reins.

"Take the U-Bahn tunnel," he said. "Go with the others. Try to get across the Spree."

Himmler turned the tyrannosaur and started to move across the chancellery garden.

"Commandant! No!" Dr. Rot ran after them. "What are you doing? Come back!"

Himmler rode off into a scene from hell; all the buildings surrounding the garden were burning, the trees shredded, black smoke billowed through the air. Everywhere were the sounds of artillery fire and exploding shells. There was the distinctive whine of a Katyusha rocket and a moment later it hit Fritz and Himmler, blowing them up in a great, bloody explosion.

Dr. Rot screamed and staggered back, shielding her face with her arms. Hot chunks of burning flame plopped on the ground all around her. The smell of blood and burning meat was overpowering. When the explosion settled to a sizzle, Dr. Rot slowly lowered her arms and looked up again. The garden was scattered with bits of burning dinosaur.

Dr. Rot emitted a sound of horror and ran.

*

Berlin was a burning skeleton of itself. Every evidence of human life was blackened and hollowed out. Shopfronts smashed, flames leaping from windows above, tramcars on their side, wheels piteously exposed, cars burned to shells and on their backs like dead bugs. Russian soldiers crouched behind the corners of buildings, firing their sub-machine guns, throwing grenades. Therizinosaurs prowled through the black smoke, flushing terrified Berliners from cellars and alleyways to be rounded up by the Russians and evacuated.

A woman ran, disoriented down a burning street, dodging from ruin to ruin, coughing from the smoke and dust. Her bleached hair and white coat were now black with soot, her blackened face streaked white with tears. Flattening herself against a wall in danger of collapsing, she paused as something caught her eye. Dr. Rot squinted through the smoke.

Two juvenile tyrannosaurs darted across the street each with a German soldier on its back. The first one made it into a side street. The second soldier got shot and fell from the saddle.

Hugging the side of a building, Dr. Rot staggered forward. She recognized the second tyrannosaur, the largest and best fed of the pod.

"Adolfi!" she called to it.

A bullet hit the wall over her head and bits of brick exploded off. Dr. Rot threw herself to the filthy sidewalk and played dead. Bullets pinged and cracked precariously close as she lay with her face in the grit.

Hearing the bullets move off half a block, Dr. Rot got to her knees and crawled forward.

"Adolfi!" she called again. "Adolfi!" She coughed, inhaling black smoke, her eyes streaming. She could hardly hear her own voice over the continuous shelling. Grit and chunks of mortar rained down on her, hitting her in the back but Dr. Rot crawled like a determined animal.

Riderless, Adolfi drifted into the relative safety of a half-collapsed building. Scrambling over piles of bricks and burning beams, Dr. Rot followed him.

"Adolfi!"

At last, Dr. Rot reached him. The tyrannosaur was more interested in nibbling a dead body at its feet.

"Down, Adolfi! Down!"

Obediently, Adolfi squatted and Dr. Rot awkwardly clambered into the saddle with bloody hands and knees. Gathering the reins of chain, she cried, "Go! Go!" and kicked mercilessly. They darted forward into a side street, a shell hitting the corner of the building they just passed, bricks and mortar exploding.

*

Dr. Rot was lost. The Fuhrer was dead. Himmler was dead. Fritz smoldered in bits amidst the ruins of the chancellery garden. Berlin was lost. And Dr. Rot was lost. She threw caution to the wind and charged down the street on Adolfi, *Pickelhaube* helmet pointy and straight, sword unsheathed and whacking Adolfi to make him go faster. White sheets hung in surrender from the buildings around her. Skirting Adolfi's feet were hay carts full of wounded. The rubble of a collapsed building blocked the street and Adolfi clambered over the wreckage with ease, continuing on at a run.

A small Berlin square... Dr. Rot reined in for a moment, looking around, disoriented. The sound of exploding shells was particularly intense, the smoke billowing so thickly Dr. Rot coughed and strained to see through the haze. She turned Adolfi uncertainly one way, then another, then randomly forged ahead.

The air was full of flashes, fire, exploding shells, the square littered with craters, debris from barricades, bullet-riddled vehicles. A water-filled trench from a collapsed tunnel also cut through the square. Running across this battlefield were divisions of Russian soldiers and therizinosaurs. Many were falling in the cross-fire.

Frantic, shrieking, Dr. Rot sharply turned Adolfi and fled behind the perimeter of the square. She didn't go ten paces further, however, before she saw something alarming in her path and reined in again. A large shape shrouded by smoke stood still amid all the noise and chaos. As the haze thinned for a moment the shape of a therizinosaur appeared. Between the great billows of smoke Dr. Elsa Wild was visible on the dinosaur's back.

Dr. Rot gasped, terrified. It wasn't possible... she was here! The traitor! For just a moment Dr. Rot forgot her terror as she beheld this former colleague in that ridiculous American uniform and helmet.

Slowly, Elsa rode forward, her therizinosaur hissing and threateningly raising its great claws at the sight of the tyrannosaur.

"Do you know where you are?" Dr. Rot heard the woman say before another blast rendered speech impossible. Elsa was riding forward. "This is the Konigsplatz," Elsa resumed. "The Reichstag is burning behind you."

The Reichstag, a beleaguered building amid the explosions and smoke. Its towering pillars were bullet-scarred, the glass cupola smashed, the decorative statues missing heads and limbs.

"The Russians are fighting to take it," Elsa said. "When it falls, Berlin will be in their hands."

Elsa rode forward till the therizinosaur and tyrannosaur were nearly nose to nose. She stopped.

"Surrender now," Elsa raised her voice over the mortar fire. "Surrender to me! It will be better that way."

The therizinosaur hissed and swiped the air with its claws. Elsa controlled it with the reins. The young tyrannosaur snapped his jaws.

"No!" Dr. Rot cried, her voice swallowed up in the din.

"It's finished, Griselda!" Elsa hollered. "Germany is defeated!"

"*No!*" Dr. Rot screamed.

She brought her sword down on Elsa but the therizinosaur raised its claws and deflected the blow, causing Dr. Rot to drop the sword. Adolfi then lunged at the therizinosaur, tried to bite its neck but the therizinosaur slashed him across the face. Adolfi reeled backwards with a roar. Dr. Rot momentarily lost control of the tyrannosaur which turned and ran. Adolfi charged blindly into the Konigsplatz war zone as Dr. Rot grappled with the reins.

Elsa urged her therizinosaur forward in pursuit.

Dr. Rot brought Adolfi under control and steered him along the perimeter of the Konigsplatz. Artillery fire and explosions were all around her. Elsa followed, squinting through the smoke, trying to keep Dr. Rot in sight. Dr. Rot reined in Adolfi for just a moment, glancing about disorientedly, trying to get her bearings. She spied something.

The Kroll Opera House; its Grecian roofline hung with tattered Nazi flags, the gargoyles staring with blank eyes at the Götterdämmerung below. Dr. Rot urged Adolfi forward again and made for the building.

Adolfi leaped over craters, shouldered mangled sleeper cars out of the way, ducked low under flying bullets, and reached the wall of the building. Dr. Rot rode along the side of it, trying to find a way in until she found a smashed, arched window and steered Adolfi into it. She just managed to squeeze the tyrannosaur through.

In the dim interior of a side lobby, the carpet was covered with shattered glass, the walls were cracked. Adolfi's body nearly filled the width of the lobby. He ducked low to avoid the ceiling. Dr. Rot urged him along, emitting a shriek when she banged her helmet against one of the small chandeliers. She steered Adolfi through a pair of double doors to the left.

Adolfi got stuck halfway through. Dr. Rot kicked him to force him on and with much wriggling Adolfi squeezed in, tearing the doors off their hinges. Dr. Rot rode him down the center aisle, his body scraping against the chairs. Halfway down the aisle she stopped and, gasping and panting, slid ungracefully out of the saddle, half falling into a chair.

The theater of the Kroll Opera House, the plenary hall of the Reichstag. Part of the roof was blown away, shafts of smoky sunlight illuminated the interior. It was a relative oasis of peace from the chaos outside, the sounds of battle were muffled here.

Dr. Rot stared blankly, stupefied with exhaustion. A strange place, she thought absently. Part government building, part entertainment venue, the red velvet curtains and gold gilt clashed with the austere – enormous – eagle that hung over the stage, a huge swastika clutched in its talons. Equally huge Nazi flags flanked the stage on either wall, wafting tiredly in the sooty air. The eagle had come loose and hung at an absurd slant, held up only by one wing. The once brilliantly gold curtain behind it was torn and tattered.

Dr. Rot straightened her helmet. The pounding continued outside, regularly shaking the theater and sending down a continuous rain of crystals from the chandelier. The prisms clinked down all around her and bounced off the *Pickelhaube*, a gentle little tinkling in contrast to the violent noise beyond. Adolfi wandered, crunching over chairs, the clanking of his reins accompaniment to the tinkling crystals.

Dimly, Dr. Rot heard the sound of a door opening and closing. Adolfi snapped to. Dr. Rot sat up, startled. She heard heavy, ponderous footsteps. But no intruder was visible.

Adolfi was very still, listening intently. A shell exploded outside, shaking the opera house. The chandelier vibrated violently at the impact and the tinkling rain of crystals became hail. Bits of plaster broke loose from the painted ceiling. Then silence except for the muffled artillery fire. The heavy footsteps started again.

"Who's there?" Dr. Rot shrieked, half rising. "Who is it? I'm armed!"

She felt for her sword only to remember it was lost.

From the shadows near the orchestra pit, out of the murky dimness, emerged Elsa Wild, leading her therizinosaur by the reins, minus the saddle.

Dr. Rot froze in fear.

With the reins, Elsa pulled down the therizinosaur's head and removed them with the bridle. Then, Elsa moved out of the way.

Hissing, claws aloft, the therizinosaur advanced up the center aisle.

Dr. Rot screamed and scrambled deeper into the sea of chairs, tripping, falling.

"Adolfi!" she screamed. "Adolfi! Attack! Kill!"

The tyrannosaur and therizinosaur faced off over the sea of chairs, Adolfi lowering himself into fighting stance, the therizinosaur pulling itself up and spreading its claws. Then the therizinosaur shrieked and charged, stomping over the chairs, neck out, eyes blazing. Adolfi hissed and lunged at the charging therizinosaur, his maw gaping, head angled to bite.

The two dinosaurs slammed together as the wooden chairs cracked and snapped beneath their feet. The therizinosaur screamed and slashed. Red streaks appeared on Adolfi's face. The sauropod ducked beneath Adolfi's snapping jaws, cutting the tyrannosaur on the chest. The tyrannosaur roared in rage and staggered back into a first-tier balcony, knocking out the support pillar, sending an entire section of balcony crashing down. Dust and chunks of plaster swirled up; red velvet curtains fluttered.

Adolfi barreled sideways over the chairs, his tail taking out another pillar, more balconies collapsed, and the therizinosaur rushed forward to meet him, claws red. The tyrannosaur ripped up half a row of chairs and flung them at the therizinosaur. They sailed across the theater with the lightness of confetti, banging down around the therizinosaur like small bombs, hitting the smaller dinosaur, pinning it beneath.

In two strides Adolfi crunched over the mangled seating area, jaws gaping, and moved in for the kill. With one free claw the therizinosaur slashed at Adolfi's head and kicked off the broken chairs as the tyrannosaur reeled back, roaring in rage.

Elsa slipped out into the side lobby. She steadied herself against the wall as a nearby explosion nearly knocked her off her feet. Then, moving along the wall, she found a door, opened it, and entered one of the opera boxes. There, just to the left of the stage, she watched the battle.

The theater shook from outside mortar fire and crashing dinosaurs within. Adolfi and the therizinosaur wrestled and slammed into walls, opera boxes falling around them as Dr. Rot ran screaming up and down a side aisle.

Now, both dinosaurs were bloodied. Panting with exertion, their ribs heaving, the tyrannosaur and therizinosaur circled each other over the flattened and splintered chairs. Dust floated through the shafts of light, all around them the interior of the theater was shattered. The dangling chandelier was swinging, groaning, and tinkling.

The dinosaurs threw themselves at each other once more with doubled ferocity. Decorative statues were shaken loose, toppled from their niches high above like unconscious divers and crashed to the floor.

Dr. Rot crouched by the railing of the orchestra pit. A huge statue crashed down beside her, missing her by inches, splintered floorboards flying up. Deafened, whimpering, she scrambled over the railing and fell ungracefully into the orchestra pit.

Falling from a few feet above onto chairs and music stands, she pulled herself to her feet and ducked through a door leading backstage.

In Elsa's box seat, debris rained down before her. She shielded her face with her arms and backed further away.

Backstage at the opera house, there was little light except for one of two shafts from the broken roof. Dr. Rot stumbled through. In the wings of the stage, she paused, listening to the dinosaur battle raging outside.

In the theater, Adolfi was the worse for wear, covered with dust and blood, encumbered by his saddle and reins. Claws red with blood, the therizinosaur advanced on him. Adolfi was exhausted. He made a feeble biting movement and the therizinosaur made the kill, slashing the tyrannosaurus' throat.

Adolfi staggered, made a gruesome gargling noise, and tipped sideways. He fell slowly, like a tree trunk, and met the floor with a loud crunch.

Backstage, Dr. Rot heard the death rattle of her dinosaur. Outside, the battle for Berlin rumbled like distant thunder. Uncertain, carefully, Dr. Rot groped her way onto the stage and approached the gently swaying gold curtain. She parted it with her hands. Stepping through the curtain onto the apron of the stage, she regarded this Armageddon.

The theater's interior was completely destroyed, unrecognizable, the dust settled like a soft mist. Adolfi lay dead, his enormous jaws hanging open. The therizinosaur was nowhere to be seen.

Dr. Rot sadly surveyed the wreckage. The seats had been trampled to broken matchsticks, support pillars lay like fallen trees, red velvet curtains flopped over balconies, nearly white with dust. And at the center of it all, Adolfi, dead, the Fuhrer's pet, Dr. Rot's pride, ripped open in a small lake of blood.

Behind her, the huge, tilting eagle swayed slightly as something moved behind it. Dr. Rot whirled around and, horrified, saw a huge, bloody claw emerging through the torn curtain, followed by the head and neck of the therizinosaur.

"Take off the armband!" Elsa cried from the box. "He's homing in on the swastika! Take it off!"

"Never!" Dr. Rot clapped a hand over it.

"Just rip it off! Quickly! He'll stop!"

"Never! You traitor!"

"Surrender to me! Please, Griselda!"

"No! ...No!" Dr. Rot shrieked, letting go of her arm and swinging her fist uselessly at the bloody claw.

The therizinosaur slashed, cutting red tears across her face and body. Then he slashed with his other claw. The red tears crisscrossed over each other. He slashed a third time. Dr. Rot fell.

With a muted thud into the floorboards, it was over. The therizinosaur wandered back behind the curtain like an actor exiting a violent revenge drama. Dr. Rot lay shriveled and small in death, her lab coat stained with bright red stripes.

Elsa sat alone in the smashed theater with the dead tyrannosaur, Dr. Rot a bloodied, white heap on the stage. Silence, except for the muffled gunfire from the

Konigsplatz. Elsa sadly regarded her former colleague, a brilliant woman who had chosen the wrong way, who had joined hands with a monster, created monsters, and died at the hands of one. How small and shriveled she was in death, lying just below the tilted swastika clutched in the eagle's talons.

Then, the huge, slanting eagle gave way and fell to the floor with a loud metallic clank, tipping forward over Dr. Rot and covering her with its metal wings.

*

The Russian flag was raised over the burned-out Reichstag. In the *Konigsplatz,* Russian soldiers cheered atop their tanks. The ground was littered with dead soldiers. With them, amid the trash of war, the craters, the shell casings, the burned vehicles, the decapitated heads from the caryatids atop the Reichstag, lay the fallen therizinosaurs.

Quietly moving through the square, ignoring the noise of victory, Dr. Elsa Wild rode on her dinosaur with the bloody claws.

In the ensuing days, the women of Berlin were formed into long lines and began passing buckets. Buckets upon buckets upon buckets, slowly clearing away the rubble of war. Other lines of women passed pipes and bits of machinery to freight trains headed for Russia. Later, some of them would remember seeing four mid-sized tyrannosaurs – or was it three, the number varied – loaded into another freight car which then departed east. It was observed that the young tyrannosaurs' flanks were now branded with the hammer and sickle.

CHAPTER XVI

Camp Mesozoic, Florida, 1950

A TV news announcer stood on the grounds of Camp Mesozoic. Behind him loomed the huge Resurrection Lab.

"Welcome to Florida, ladies and gentlemen. This is Brett Conway, reporting to you from Camp Mesozoic, home of the world-renowned research project that gave America its fighting dinosaurs. Five years after the end of the war it is still a fully active facility, continuing its search into past eons, reanimating dinosaurs so that we in the present day will more fully understand these fascinating creatures.

"And with me here today is someone very special that I want you to meet, Dr. Elsa Wild, the German émigré who defied Hitler and brought her invaluable knowledge of dinosaur reanimation, known as *Dino...lebhaf...tig...keit* to America."

Elsa moved into view next to Brett.

"And this is her husband, Dr. Robert Gorman, paleontologist, with their four-year-old daughter, Heidi." Dr. Gorman, holding a little girl, moved in on the other side of the announcer. The little girl smiled and waved. "They join with the rest of America this day to witness the unveiling of Camp Mesozoic's latest creation."

Brett Conway held the microphone before Elsa.

"Dr. Wild," he said, "tell us what we're going to see today."

Elsa leaned in towards the microphone.

"Today," she said, a little nervous before the camera, "we are unveiling to the public a Paleozoic-era sea scorpion."

"A scorpion," said Brett. "So, today's prehistoric creature is somewhat smaller than your usual fare."

"Relatively smaller. Camp Mesozoic is expanding its research into prehistoric sea creatures, something which we have not focused on until now. We have installed a saltwater tank in the Resurrection Lab."

"There has been some debate in scientific circles, Dr. Wild," said Brett, "about the wisdom of reanimating creatures that you may not be able to control."

"That has never been a problem at Camp Mesozoic," Elsa assured him. "All our research here is very carefully controlled."

"At Camp Mesozoic, perhaps, but what about the safety of the larger society? The German tyrannosaurs that were taken to Russia after the war, for example. No one knows what happened to them, how they are being used inside the Soviet Union. Your science of –" Brett referred to his notes "–*Dino...leb...haftig...keit* fell into enemy hands."

"The German *Dinolebhaftigkeit* fell into enemy hands during the chaos at the end of the war. American *Dinolebhaftigkeit* is secure; no American therizinosaurs fell into enemy hands."

"Are you sure, Dr. Wild? There have been reports that some therizinosaurs were taken by fleeing Nazis to other countries. A Nazi dinosaur breeding program could resume in the jungles of Africa or South America."

"Those reports have not been confirmed," Elsa answered him. "The Russians may or may not still have the tyrannosaurs but they do not have the process of *Dinolebhaftigkeit.*"

"But you must admit," Brett persisted, "there is some danger that this *Dino...figkeit* or one of your animals could fall into the wrong hands. The result for society could be disastrous."

"There is always some risk involved in scientific research. But I believe scientific advance outweighs the risk."

"Thank you, Dr. Wild." Elsa moved out of shot. "And now, ladies and gentlemen, I believe the presentation of the sea scorpion is about to begin."

Elsa, Robert Gorman, and Heidi sat in makeshift bleachers with a phalanx of the press. News cameras were set up to record this momentous event and newspaper reporters leaned forward, notebooks at the ready, photographers focused their lenses. Elsa took Heidi into her lap.

The bleachers were arranged on either side of the enormous, sliding doors of the Resurrection Lab. Was this too close? The reporters murmured among themselves. Was it safe? Who knew what a prehistoric scorpion might do? The doors started to slide open. The murmurs of concern changed to murmurs of expectation. The doors opened all the way. It was black within. Then, the thing started to crawl out into the sunlight.

Through the hangar door, the armored arachnid head emerged, then two huge pincer claws. Gasps went up from the spectators. The thing kept coming, its two-foot-wide, armored body, the crooked legs, two, four, six. Some members of the press jumped off the bleachers, swearing. It continued to crawl out, its armored tail finishing its seven-foot length. Then it paused, moving its tail, flexing its legs. Exclamations and cries of fear came from the spectators.

Dr. Gorman looked askance – but amazed – at this monster. Elsa smiled proudly. She rose, holding her daughter, so that Heidi had a better view. Heidi grinned and clapped her hands with delight.

"Ya-a-a-a-a-ay!" she enthused, clapping.

On the ground, between the two sets of bleachers, the enormous, black arachnid crouched very still, its exoskeleton shining in the bright, Florida sunshine. A few photographers began snapping pictures. Other reporters, obeying some primeval instinct, kept their distance and looked on, incredulous.

Then, slowly, the scorpion raised its terrifying pincers... and opened them.

Cries of alarm turned to screams as more reporters bailed off the bleachers. Elsa remained unperturbed and drew Heidi's attention to the scorpion's claws.

"Is she crazy?" a reporter from the Florida Sun Times exclaimed.

"She's insane!" cried a columnist from the New York Times.

"You can't trust a Kraut!" hollered the science writer for the Seattle Sun. "Never should have let her into this country! *What is she doing?*"

"Someone shoot that thing!" a voice called out.

"She's just standing there with her daughter!" The voices began to blend into a general howl of outrage. "What kind of mother is this? ...Fool woman! ...She can't control it! ...Get a gun! Who's got a gun? Where's the goddam security?"

One TV cameraman remained calm and filmed Brett Conway running towards the gates of Camp Mesozoic, screaming, "The war is over, shut this place down!"

Some said that Dr. Wild's hearing hadn't been so good since the Battle of Berlin, which was why the noise didn't touch her now. Some called her a megalomaniac. Some swore they never trusted her.

Elsa Wild stood, serene amid the chaos – but weren't her creatures born for chaos? – and smiled upon her creation.

THE END

Check out other great

Dinosaur Thrillers!

Steve Metcalf

OBJEKT 221

Ruthless multi-national conglomerate Allied Genetics is under siege from a paramilitary force for hire. Allied calls in reinforcements and fortifies their crown-jewel property – an abandoned Soviet military facility in Crimea known during the Cold War as Objekt 221. Fortunately for the future of their research, O221 straddles a stretch of rocky landscape that hides a rift – a portal through time and space. Through this rift, Allied Genetics can travel, at will, to the Cretaceous – 100 million years into Earth's past – and bolster their genetic experiments with dinosaur DNA ... something their competitors want to stop at all costs."Objekt 221" is a story blending numerous science fiction elements such as repurposed military facilities, time travel, rogue corporate armies, dinosaurs and the hint of a super-ancient civilization.

Bestselling collection

PREHISTORIC:
A DINOSAUR ANTHOLOGY

PREHISTORIC is an action packed collection of stories featuring terrifying creatures that once ruled the Earth. Lost worlds where T-Rex and Velociraptors still roam and man is now on the menu. Laboratories at the forefront of cloning technology experiment with dinosaurs they do not understand or are able to contain. The deepest parts of the ocean where Megalodon, the largest and most ferocious predator to have ever existed is stalking new prey. Plus many more thrillers filled with extinct prehistoric monsters written by some of the best creature feature authors this side of the Jurassic period.

Check out other great

Dinosaur Thrillers!

Julian Michael Carver

TRIASSIC

After spending many years in artificial hypersleep, a handful of survivors of the exploration vessel Supernova awaken to find their ship torn to shreds. They are unsure of what happened in space or how they crashed into an uncharted planet. Upon exploration of the new world, they soon realize their destination: The Triassic, the first chapter of the Mesozoic Era. A plan is formulated to escape this terrifying landscape plagued with dinosaurs and prehistoric beasts. The survivors soon discover that there may be an even larger threat looming under the trees than just the dinosaurs, threatening to cut their mission short and trap them all forever in the primitive depths of the Triassic.

Hugo Navikov

THE FOUND WORLD

A powerful global cabal wants adventurer Brett Russell to retrieve a superweapon stolen by the scientist who built it. To entice him to travel underneath one of the most dangerous volcanoes on Earth to find the scientist, this shadowy organization will pay him the only thing he cares about: information that will allow him to avenge his family's murder. But before he can get paid, he and his team must enter an underground hellscape of killer plants, giant insects, terrifying dinosaurs, and an army of other predators never previously seen by man. At the end of this journey awaits a revelation that could alter the fate of mankind ... if they can make it back from this horrifying found world.

Check out other great

Dinosaur Thrillers!

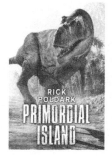

Rick Poldark

PRIMORDIAL ISLAND

During a violent storm Flight 207 crash-lands in the South China Sea. Poseidon Tech tracks the wreckage to an uncharted island and dispatches a curious salvage team—two paleontologists, a biologist specializing in animal behavior, a botanist, and a nefarious big game hunter. Escorted by a heavily-armed security team, they cut through the jungle and quickly find themselves in a terrifying fight for survival, running a deadly gauntlet of prehistoric predators. In their quest for the flight recorder, they uncover the mystery of the island's existence and discover an arcane force that will tip the balance of power on the primordial island. Things are not as they seem as they race against time to survive the island's man-eating dinosaurs and make it back home in one piece.

P.K. Hawkins

SUBTERRANEA

Fall, 1985. The small town of Kettle Hollow barely shows up on any maps, and four young friends are used to taking their BMX's outside of town in an effort to find anything interesting to do. But tonight their tendency to go off by themselves may have saved them, and also forced them into the adventure of a lifetime.While they were away, Kettle Hollow has been locked down by the government, and a portal to another world has opened on Main Street. It's a world deep below the ground, a world where dinosaurs roam free, where giant plants and mutant insects hunt for prey. It's also a world where all their family and friends have been kidnapped for sinister purposes. Now, with time running out before the portal closes, the four friends must brave the unknown to save their loved ones. Time is running out, and in the darkened tunnels of Subterranea, something is hunting them.